D

P9-DYZ-911

THE CHOCOLATE BRIDAL BASH

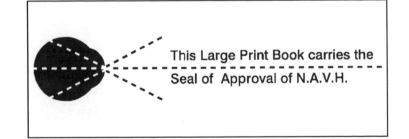

This Large Print Book carries the
Seal of Approval of N.A.V.H.

A CHOCOHOLIC MYSTERY

THE CHOCOLATE BRIDAL BASH

JoAnna Carl

THORNDIKE PRESS

An imprint of Thomson Gale, a part of The Thomson Corporation

THOMSON

GALE

Detroit • New York • San Francisco • New Haven, Conn. • Waterville, Maine • London

THOMSON

™

GALE

LIBRARY OF CONGRESS CATALOGING-IN-PUBLICATION DATA

Carl, JoAnna.
   The chocolate bridal bash : a chocoholic mystery / by JoAnna Carl.
     p. cm. — (Thorndike Press large print mystery)
   ISBN 0-7862-9099-4 (lg. print : alk. paper) 1. Weddings — Fiction. 2. Chocolate industry — Fiction. 3. Women detectives — Michigan — Fiction. 4. Michigan — Fiction. 5. Large type books. I. Title.
PS3569.A51977C47 2006
813'.087380806—dc22   2006028952

U.S. Hardcover:
ISBN 13: 978-0-7862-9099-4
ISBN 10: 0-7862-9099-4

Published in 2006 by arrangement with NAL Signet, a member of Penguin Group (USA) Inc.

Printed in the United States of America on permanent paper
10 9 8 7 6 5 4 3 2 1

For Mary Jo Dilks.
Best friends forever.

ACKNOWLEDGMENTS

With thanks to my Michigan friends, always ready to help with background and fact-checking; to Colleen McGee and Ed McGee, who remember the 1970s, even if they were there; and to Dr. Doug Lyle, expert on violent death.

CHAPTER 1

After I overcame all my misgivings and invited my mother to my wedding, it was a little disappointing to learn that she didn't want to come.

I admit it was the place, rather than the occasion, that drew her objections.

"Warner Pier?" Her voice was so angry it could have melted every line between her phone in Texas and mine in Michigan. "You're getting married in Warner Pier? Why?"

"It's where Joe and I live," I said. "It's where we plan to continue loving — I mean, living!"

I'd pulled one of my usual stunts, tangling my tongue. I misspeak so often — they're called "malapropisms" — that most of my family and friends simply ignore my slips. Hoping my mother would do that, I went on quickly. "Warner Pier is where important parts of our families live. It's where all our friends live. Why wouldn't we want to get married here?"

My mom ignored my question. "Why not get married here in Dallas? We could plan a lovely wedding in Dallas."

"Dallas? But Dallas was never — I mean, I don't have good associations with Dallas. I know I lived there twelve years, but if people ask me where I'm from, I always say Prairie Creek."

"Podunk Creek! You and your dad, the hick! I'll never understand this compulsion you two have to live at the back of nowhere!"

I sighed. "If that's the way you feel, you'd better know the worst. Daddy has already said he's coming. And Annie is coming with him."

"I knew she wouldn't miss it!"

I ignored that. "And I've already told them I expect nice beheading — I mean, behavior! I expect nice behavior from all three of you."

"I would never ruin your wedding by quarreling with your father and that woman he married."

I sighed. "Just don't run out on me, Mom."

I'm not sure what I meant by that comment, and maybe my mom didn't know what it meant either. Her voice was calmer than it had been.

"Lee, I wouldn't run out on your wedding. Believe me, I wouldn't. I want your wedding to be perfect for you. It's just that — you know how I feel about Warner Pier."

"I know how, Mom. But I'll never understand why. Why do you dislike this town so much?"

"You've bought into the tourist view." Her voice became sarcastic. "It's a darling little Victorian resort town. A regular trip down memory lane to the good old days."

"You're forgetting the crime rate around here. I'm aware that the people of Warner Pier are like people anywhere. There's a dark side to everyone's personality. People are always — you know — doing things they shouldn't have done and leaving undone things they should have done. Seems to me that happens in Dallas, too."

"It sure happened in Warner Pier when I lived there. And in Prairie Creek, too."

Another silence grew up between us. Then my mother spoke. "Is Nettie there?"

I was calling from my office, so I put the phone down and went back into the workroom of TenHuis Chocolade ("Handmade Chocolates in the Dutch Tradition"). Most of the ladies who actually make the chocolate had left for the day, but Aunt Nettie, chocolatier deluxe and my boss, was sprinkling light brown granules of Turbinado sugar over a tray of strawberry truffles ("white chocolate and strawberry interior coated in dark chocolate").

"Aunt Nettie, your long-lost sister-in-law wants to talk to you."

"Oh, my goodness!" Aunt Nettie had reason to be surprised. My mom and I usually communicated by e-mail. If Aunt Nettie got involved, it was with a casual, "Say hi to Sally."

Aunt Nettie washed her hands, turning off the water with her elbow in health department-approved style. She headed toward the phone in the break room.

She and my mom were talking by the time I got back to the office phone, and I listened in. My mom hadn't messed around with a lot of preliminary politeness; she was asking a direct question. It was one that surprised me.

"Who's sheriff of Warner County now?" she said.

"Sheriff?" Aunt Nettie sounded puzzled. "Let me think. It's some man named Smith. I don't remember his first name."

"Then Carl Van Hoosier is out?"

"Van Hoosier? He left office years ago."

"I suppose that there's no hope that he's dead."

Aunt Nettie laughed. "I don't have the slightest idea. If he's alive, he'd be a hundred years old. I could find out."

"No! No, it's okay. I just want to make sure he's not still throwing his weight around. Lee? Are you on the line?"

"Sure am. Do you want me to hang up?"

"Oh, no. What's the date for the wedding?"

I told her, adding, "It's on a Saturday."

"Three weeks after Easter," Aunt Nettie said. "I told Lee people in the chocolate business can't take honeymoons until the last bunny's been sold."

I could almost hear my mom forcing her voice to sound cheerful. "I'll clear my schedule and plan to be there. And I'll be polite. Maybe I can come a few days early and help fill the rice bags or something."

"That would be wonderful, Mom."

She sighed again, and when she spoke her voice sounded faintly worried. "It'll be okay. I'm sure it will."

I promised to keep my mother informed on the wedding plans, and we all hung up. Then I met Aunt Nettie in the break room. I was curious. "What's the deal with this former sheriff? What did he have to do with Mom?"

"I haven't the slightest idea, Lee."

"She didn't leave town one step ahead of the law?"

Aunt Nettie laughed. "As far as I know the sheriff wasn't after her, though the minister might have been."

"The minister? Why would the minister have been concerned? I never heard of Mom darkening the door of a church."

"That was the problem, I guess. She didn't darken the door when she should have."

"What are you talking about?"

Aunt Nettie's eyes widened. "Don't you know about how your mother came to leave Warner Pier?"

"She took the bus, I guess. She always told me she wanted to see the world and could barely wait to get out of town."

"She never told you any details?"

"What details?"

"Lee, your mother ran away from Warner Pier on what was supposed to be her wedding day!"

CHAPTER 2

Aunt Nettie might as well have tossed a barrel of Lake Michigan's wintry water on me. I had never been so astonished in my life. I stood there gaping.

My mother had been engaged when she left Warner Pier? She had left on what would have been her wedding day?

How could she do that?

And how could she never have told her only daughter about it?

It was a family secret I'd never had a hint existed. I hung on to a stainless steel worktable, staring at Aunt Nettie. "Tell me all!" I said.

Unfortunately, before she could comply, there was a knock at the door. Aunt Nettie's dinner date, Warner Pier Police Chief Hogan Jones, had arrived. Aunt Nettie went to let him in, and our chance to talk was gone. But before they left, Aunt Nettie took me aside. "Hogan and I won't be late. I'll

15

tell you everything I know — and that's not a lot — when I get home."

"Wait! There's one thing I've got to know now. Who was Mom engaged to?"

A shadow fell across Aunt Nettie's face. "It's a long story."

I took a deep breath and voiced my greatest fear. "Was it anyone I know?"

"Oh, no!" The shadow on Aunt Nettie's face grew deeper. "No, you never knew him."

She once again assured me that she'd tell me what she knew when she got home. Then she and Hogan went out, leaving me in a state of shock. My mom had been engaged? She'd run off on her wedding day?

A picture of Mom climbing onto a bus wearing a wedding gown popped into my mind.

But that was silly. I did know a few things about my mom's youth, and one of them was that her father had died during her senior year in high school. His death had left the family in bad financial shape, she'd told me. But Mom had been in airline school in Dallas by the next fall. So the runaway bride episode must have happened during the summer after her senior year. If she'd been planning a wedding that soon after her father's death and when the family

16

was feeling hard up, it would have been something small — probably no elaborate wedding dress would have been involved.

But in a town the size of Warner Pier — permanent population 2,500 — even a small wedding is a major social event, or at least that was what Joe and I were finding out. Everybody from the druggist to the postmaster expected an invitation. The last-minute cancellation of a wedding would have had the town on its ear.

No wonder so many people aged fifty and older had asked me if my mother was coming to my wedding.

And no wonder Mom had never wanted to come back to Warner Pier in the thirty-three years since she had left. She would forever be remembered as the bride who didn't show up at her own wedding.

But who had the bridegroom been?

When my own dinner date, my fiancé Joe Woodyard, came to pick me up, I asked him what he knew about the whole thing.

Joe's a Warner Pier native and his mother is a Warner Pier native. In addition to having a bushel of brains, plus dark hair, bright blue eyes, and regular features that add up to yummy good looks, Joe is a natural athlete. In high school he made his mark by becoming a state wrestling champ and

17

captain of Michigan's best high school debate team in the same year. He went on to earn a law degree and fought for the underdog as a public defender. Then a bad marriage forced him to reassess his life goals and drop the practice of law for a career as what he calls an "honest craftsman," operating a shop that specializes in the restoration of antique wooden boats. But he's edged back into law; he's also part-time city attorney for Warner Pier.

Joe moves in so many circles — city government, boat owners, old high school pals — that he usually knows everything about everybody around Warner Pier. I was sure he'd know something about my mother's runaway-bride past.

But his answer was evasive. "I don't know much." His eyes sort of bounced off mine.

"But you did know something about it." I made it a statement. "Why didn't you ever mention this?"

"I tried talking about your mother a few times, thinking you'd tell me the whole story. But when you didn't seem to want to . . ."

"I didn't know the whole story! I didn't know there was a story!"

"I see that now. But at the time, I just thought you didn't want to talk about it."

18

"Do you know whom Mom was planning to marry?"

"I don't remember his name." Joe shrugged.

"Is he still around?"

"No." Joe's voice was final. "Come on, we're going to be late meeting Tony and Lindy."

Tony and Lindy Herrera were our closest friends. They both worked — Tony days and Lindy nights — and they had three school-age kids, so an evening out was a big treat for them. I didn't want to spoil it.

"Don't mention this tonight," I said to Joe. "I'd better get the family's official line from Aunt Nettie before I say the wrong thing around Warner Pier."

I admit I was absentminded at dinner, but I managed not to say anything too dumb. Oh, I talked to Lindy about a "runaway" for the wedding reception, when I meant a "runner" on the main serving table, and I told her my dad wanted to "escape" me. "I mean, escort!" I said quickly. "He says he didn't get to give me away the first time I got married, so this time he wants to take a powder. I mean, do the honors!"

My dad wasn't the only parent concerned with the second-time-around aspect of our wedding. It was also giving Joe's mom trouble — which meant she was giving us trouble.

Joe and I had both been married and divorced. We wanted our wedding to be simple — with more emphasis on meaning than on pomp. I was wearing a street-length dress, and Joe was wearing a business suit. I didn't have an engagement ring; Joe had had his mother's engagement diamond set on a wide gold ring that I planned to wear as a wedding band. Lindy and Tony would be our only attendants. The ceremony was to be held in Aunt Nettie's living room, with family only. We saw no need to have a rehearsal dinner.

The only thing that was getting out of hand was the reception. We were planning to invite all our friends to that, and it kept getting larger and more elaborate every day. Especially if Joe's mom had her way.

Joe's first wedding had been an elopement, just as mine had, so Mercy Woodyard hadn't been present. This time she wanted to be involved, but we weren't cooperating.

As soon as we picked a date, Mercy offered to give a rehearsal dinner, of course. She hadn't been too disappointed when we told her we didn't want one. As a successful insurance agent, she declared, she had plenty of money to spend on her only son's wedding, so she would be hostess for the reception.

She hadn't asked. She'd announced.

I hated this idea, and I'm happy to say that Joe did, too. I'm sure Mercy meant well, but letting her be hostess would mean we lost control of the event. Neither of us was willing to do that, and we'd tried to make it clear to her. But every time we thought we had her convinced, she popped right back with a new approach.

Aunt Nettie wasn't being a lot of help either. In the two years since I'd come to Warner Pier to be business manager for her chocolate company, I'd lived with her in a hundred-year-old house built by my great-grandfather. Aunt Nettie thought having the wedding in the family home was fine. It was giving her a good excuse for redecorating.

I didn't think this was a good idea. For one thing, I loved the old house — slightly shabby and full of hand-me-down furniture — just the way it was. Besides, there wasn't enough time to bring in paint, to order and hang new draperies, and to shop for new furniture. Not with Easter, one of the most important chocolate holidays of the year, to fit into our professional lives. But Aunt Nettie kept coming up with new ideas about updating the living room.

That night it helped me to talk the reception over with Lindy, who's been a friend since I was sixteen and who in her job as a caterer would be doing a lot of the hands-on work for the event. But the news that my mother had fled her hometown on the eve of her wedding haunted me. All through dinner I was more concerned about what Aunt Nettie was going to tell me than about socializing with Lindy and Tony.

So I asked Joe to take me home right after dinner, and I invited him to stay and learn the family secrets from Aunt Nettie.

"No, thanks," he said. "Aunt Nettie may want to tell you something that's not fit for masculine ears. I'll call you tomorrow."

He gave me a big kiss and held me for a long moment. "Don't worry," he said. "I'm sure Nettie will make everything clear."

Over coffee and Baileys Irish Cream bonbons — yes, Aunt Nettie and I work with chocolate all day, then eat it at home — Aunt Nettie told me about my mom's adventures as a runaway bride.

"I want to warn you that I don't know a lot," she said. "All this happened the year Phil and I started TenHuis Chocolade. We lived over the shop, and we might as well have lived inside it. We were the only two employees, and we worked night and day.

We had to. If we hadn't made a success of it that summer, we would have had to give up the idea of having a chocolate shop in Warner Pier or anywhere else — ever. So when your grandfather died, we were not a lot of help to your grandmother and Sally. Looking back, I see that Sally was in a dangerous emotional state, but at the time all I could think about was making and selling chocolate."

She sighed. "If we hadn't failed to help Sally, maybe things would have been different."

I patted her hand. "She must have been a prickly teenager."

"Well, Sally and her mother were at odds all the time. Phil was ten years older than Sally, and he felt that he had to take his mother's part, so that put Sally at odds with us. Mother TenHuis was terribly shocked by your grandfather's death — we all were. I guess we felt that Sally should carry on bravely and support her mother. We didn't really notice that she also needed support. But the arguments with her mother were getting worse all the time; I'll admit we were relieved when she and Bill Dykstra told us they were going to get married."

"Bill Dykstra? That was her fiancé's name? There are lots of Dykstras around here. You said I didn't know him, but do I know any of his relatives?"

Aunt Nettie's eyes dodged mine. "I don't think you do," she said. Then she went on with her story.

Bill Dykstra had been my mom's high school sweetheart, Aunt Nettie explained. She described him as "a nice boy," two years older than Mom. He'd just finished a two-year course in electronics at a Holland technical school. That branch of the Dykstra family was "hardworking," rather than wealthy, she said. Bill's mother had been a science teacher. His father was an electrician, and like many local craftsmen in the Warner Pier area, he also opened and closed cottages for the summer people — the people who own the hundreds of vacation homes on the shore of Lake Michigan and in the countryside around Warner Pier.

Like my mom, Bill had been eager to leave Warner Pier and see the world. He had landed a job in Chicago, and the two of them had been excited about moving to the big city. Their wedding had been scheduled for the first Sunday in August at the Warner Pier Reformed Church.

"It wasn't going to be large," Aunt Nettie said. "Just the immediate families and a few friends. None of us had any money. Your

24

grandmother hadn't worked in the thirty years since she got married, but with your grandfather gone, she was trying to find a job. She was also trying to sell your grandfather's service station. Phil and I were barely scraping by. Sally had been working as a waitress that summer, but she didn't have much money saved. I think Sally was disappointed at not having a big wedding, but she could see that it was smarter to save what money she and Bill had to set up their apartment in Chicago. The church did give her a shower, but her wedding wasn't getting too much attention."

Aunt Nettie sounded apologetic. But I could understand the way she and Uncle Phil must have felt. They had had their hands full with a new business and his recently widowed mother. Turning the responsibility for a rebellious younger sister over to a young man who seemed pleasant and reliable and whose family was "hardworking" — it could have been the answer to a prayer. They hadn't worried a lot about whether or not my mom was making the right decision.

Then, at four a.m. on what would have been the day of the wedding, my grandmother had called Uncle Phil and Aunt Nettie to say Sally hadn't come home.

"Phil and I weren't too worried," Aunt Nettie said. "After all, it was Sally and Billy's wedding day, and we thought they'd simply — well, spent the night somewhere. But your grandmother was more puritanical. She was also hysterical. Phil tried to calm her down, but we finally had to get up, get dressed, and go out to the house — this house — to talk to her. That's when we discovered Sally had taken a lot of her clothes with her."

The clothes had been packed up, ready to be moved to Chicago, Aunt Nettie said. Getting several boxes and a suitcase out of the house without disturbing a nervous mother would not have been easy, but my mom had managed it — Aunt Nettie said my grandmother might have taken a sleeping pill. The wedding dress — street-length, with an Empire waistline and lace sleeves that puffed at the top and were tight down the rest of the arm — had been left hanging in the closet.

It was Phil who found her note. My mom had left it in the kitchen cupboard, propped against the coffeepot. "Bill and I have called the wedding off for now," it read. "I'm going on to Chicago. I'll write when I find a place to stay."

There was no apology, no explanation.

26

I had never known my grandmother — she died before I was born — but I could imagine the hysterical scene Uncle Phil and Aunt Nettie had on their hands.

Aunt Nettie tried to comfort my grandmother, and Uncle Phil called Bill Dykstra's house. Surely Bill would be there and would tell them what had happened, would provide some explanation, they thought.

When Bill's parents heard the news, his dad rushed to Bill's room, eager for information. But Bill's room was empty. Bill had also disappeared — without leaving a note, even one as cryptic as my mother's had been.

Now there were two sets of frantic parents. Friends and relatives were called in. The roads of western Michigan were thick with people looking for Sally and Bill — either alone or together.

"It was late in the morning when someone thought to check the bus station in South Haven," Aunt Nettie said. "Then we found out that a girl matching your mother's description had gotten on the seven a.m. bus headed south."

"I guess that was a sort of relief," I said. "Did you have someone meet the bus in Chicago?"

"The bus had already arrived in Chicago

27

by that time. We didn't know where Sally was for six months."

"My grandmother must have been nearly crazy! But what about Bill? Had he gone with her?"

Aunt Nettie didn't answer.

"Did he turn up?" I asked.

"His father found him late that morning."

"Did Bill have any explanation for the whole thing?"

Aunt Nettie shook her head.

"No explanation? No excuse? What *did* he have to say?"

Aunt Nettie looked at me with eyes that were full of grief. "Bill couldn't say anything," she said. "His father found his car parked on a back road. A garden hose had been stretched from his exhaust into the driver's window. The engine had run until the gas tank was empty."

"Oh, no!"

"Yes. Bill had committed suicide."

CHAPTER 3

I could feel tears welling in my eyes. "How horrible," I said. "Those poor parents."

"Yes, it was awful for Bill's parents. They had two boys — Bill and his older brother, Ed. Ed — well, Ed had protested the Vietnam War, the draft. He was a real rebel. He wasn't around then because he had gone to Canada. He'd been a terrible worry to them for years. Bill had been the 'good' boy."

"It would have been awful for my grandmother, too."

"She really never recovered. Losing her husband in May, then her daughter in August . . . True, she and Sally communicated after that, but their relationship hadn't been very strong anyway, and they never became close."

"And I'm sure a lot of people around here blamed Mom for Bill's suicide."

Aunt Nettie frowned. "It's always a 'chicken or egg' question. Did Bill commit suicide because Sally left, and he was upset? Or did Sally leave because she sensed some basic instability in Bill and decided she'd better not marry him? I leaned toward that explanation."

"Has Mom ever told you her side of the story?"

"No! As I said, Sally didn't contact anyone for six months. Then she called Phil. She told him she had enrolled in airline school in Dallas, but she refused to give him her address. And she refused to talk to her mom for six months after that."

"Do you think she blamed her mother in some way?"

"I think she was ashamed to talk to her."

"When Mom called, had she even heard about what had happened to Bill?"

"Yes, she had. But she never told anybody how she found out."

"It wasn't in the newspaper?"

"Just an obituary in the *Warner Pier Gazette.* The Chicago or even the Grand Rapids papers wouldn't be interested in the suicide of an obscure young electronics repairman on a back road in rural Michigan."

"What happened to Bill's family?"

"His dad died about five years after this happened. I have no idea what became of the brother."

"How about the mother?"

"Vita Dykstra? Oh, she still lives here." Aunt Nettie got up and began to collect the cups that had held our coffee.

"But you say I don't know her."

"You've probably seen her on the street or at the Superette, but I can't think of any reason you would have met her." Aunt Nettie yawned rather ostentatiously. "And now I'm going to bed. But first, Lee, I had one more idea about what to do to the living room windows for the wedding."

"Aunt Nettie! We don't have time for you to order draperies! And it's not necessary."

"Oh, this would be simple. We could do it ourselves."

"When? In between the Easter rush and the Mother's Day rush?"

"It would only take an afternoon. We buy fabric, and we hem the edges so it's long panels. Then we get wooden drapery rods — I'm sure Joe wouldn't mind putting them up — and we simply drape the panels over the rods, letting them hang down on one end." Aunt Nettie smiled confidently. "Wouldn't that look pretty?"

"Maybe. But it wouldn't look like home. And I want to get married at home. If you want new window treatments, please wait until I move out."

Aunt Nettie laughed, and I realized she hadn't been making a serious suggestion. She had been dodging questions about Bill's mother.

So I quit asking questions and started turning out the lights, ready to go to bed myself. But I had one final comment. "Unless Mom decides to tell her side of the story," I said, "I guess it will remain a mystery."

"Mystery!" Aunt Nettie suddenly looked scared. "Don't call it a mystery!"

"Why not? It is one."

"But we know what happened."

"But we don't know why."

Aunt Nettie crossed the room and gripped my hand. "Lee, please restrain that curiosity of yours. Please don't try to find out what happened."

"I wouldn't do any more than ask Mom."

"Don't! This whole affair was a terrible mess, a tragedy. It was heartbreaking. Please don't open it up again."

I gave her a hug. "Don't worry," I said.

I lay awake a long time that night. Aunt Nettie had called the situation a tragedy and that was exactly the word for it. Bill Dykstra — by her account a nice young man — had died. My mother had left home and had apparently felt too ashamed to come back again. As far as I knew she'd only returned to Warner Pier once in the thirty-plus years since she'd left. Her mother had been buried in Grand Rapids, and Mom had shown up, I knew, but that was still sixty miles from here. She *had* come to Warner Pier for Uncle Phil's funeral, but stayed only a few days. I'd been along on that trip. I remembered that Mom refused to leave the house, even to go to the grocery store.

The effect on my grandmother and on Bill's parents had also been dramatic. My grandmother had "never recovered," Aunt Nettie had said.

Apparently Warner Pier hadn't gotten over it, either. At least a dozen people who were longtime residents had asked about my mother. I hadn't thought a lot about that until now. I guess I had felt that their curiosity was based on friendly memories. Now I wondered if that was true.

As I drifted off to sleep, I thought about Mrs. Dykstra. Vita, Aunt Nettie had called her. She still lived in Warner Pier. I wondered what her life was like. How had she coped? Had the scapegrace son, Ed, ever returned from Canada? Apparently he didn't live in Warner Pier.

Aunt Nettie obviously didn't want to talk

about Mrs. Dykstra. But maybe Joe or his mother — both Warner Pier natives — would be willing to tell me.

Aunt Nettie had urged me not to look into the whole affair. I could see why she didn't want me to. But I hadn't promised that I wouldn't.

Next morning I called Joe at his boat shop and invited him to lunch. "I'll meet you at the Sidewalk Café," I said. "My treat."

"Oh, I can buy lunch," Joe said. "I made some headway on the credit cards this month. And in less than three months I'm going to have a professional accountant take over my personal finances."

"Ha! Today I'm not feeling financially savvy. We can go dutch. I'll see you at the Sidewalk at one."

I do have a degree in accounting. When Joe and I met, nearly two years earlier, he'd been in terrible financial shape — saddled with debts incurred in starting up the boat shop and unable to access money he'd invested jointly with his ex-wife. He'd been living in a back room at the boat shop, with his mortgage weighing on him like an anchor and his credit card debt as high as the clouds over Lake Michigan.

Then his ex-wife was killed, and Joe discovered that she'd never changed the will she made while they were married. He inherited what appeared to be a substantial fortune. This turned out to be more of a bane than a blessing, since her debts were also substantial, and Joe was determined not to benefit financially from his legacy. Her affairs were such a mess that it had taken him a year to get things on the road to some sort of order.

Just the previous fall he'd presented his ex-wife's Warner Pier estate to the city for use as a conference center. In typical Joe fashion, he'd forbidden any official recognition of his gift. He still had to live frugally; he relied on his small salary as part-time city attorney to pay the rent on an apartment over an antique shop on Warner Pier's main street.

But I was making a good salary, now that TenHuis Chocolade's financial situation was improving. Joe and I believed that we could do all right if we pooled our financial resources.

I had been watching the clock, but a half hour before I was to meet Joe I got a call from the buyer for a Detroit gift shop. She wanted information before she could place her Easter order. TenHuis makes a lot of money selling fancy bunnies to her, so I talked to Aunt Nettie about ordering special packaging, and the two of us went back to my office to do a little arithmetic on pricing. I'd almost forgotten my lunch date when I heard a loud clatter from outside our front window — my office is glass-enclosed and overlooks the workshop, our retail area, and beyond that, Peach Street, Warner Pier's main drag.

The noise got my attention, and I looked out and saw a ramshackle truck loaded with garbage bags. An old woman in a dirty white stocking cap with an enormous red pom-pom had just dropped a similar bag, and dozens of aluminum cans were rolling around on the sidewalk.

"Oh, gosh!" I said aloud. "Lovie's scattered a million cans all over the sidewalk."

Lovie — I didn't know her last name — was a well-known figure around Warner Pier. She collected aluminum cans for recycling, following a regular route. Her presence and way of life in our little resort town had always amazed me. Warner Pier won't even allow McDonald's in the town on the grounds that it would be an eyesore in our pristine Victorian community. But nobody ever complained about Lovie, her sacks of cans, her rattletrap truck, and her falling-down junk shop out on the highway.

My report on the scattered cans made

Aunt Nettie look stricken. "Don't say anything to her!"

"I won't, since you don't want me to, though I don't understand why Warner Pier merchants put up with her and her junk. But I'm late to lunch. I'll call about the Detroit bunnies after you figure the packaging cost."

Aunt Nettie nodded, and I got my ski jacket and left. I would have hurried down the block to the Sidewalk Café if I could have gotten through the cans outside the shop without kicking them out of the way. But I couldn't. The old woman in the cap with the red pom-pom was picking them up slowly. I simply couldn't walk by her and ignore them.

"Here, Lovie, let me help you," I said.

"No need, pretty girl! I'm not so old that I can't pick up a few cans."

"You hold the sack open, and I'll dump 'em in," I said.

But Lovie didn't pay any attention to me. She didn't spurn my efforts to help, but she wouldn't cooperate either. I'd pick up a couple of cans, and I'd almost have to snatch the big black plastic bag away from her to return them to her stash. It was very frustrating. My shoulder bag was swinging around, I was digging cans out of the slush in the gutter and almost slipping on icy patches near the curb. And I was late to lunch with the man I loved.

Then I heard Joe's voice. "Here, Lovie," he said. "Mom sent these over."

Joe had appeared from the direction of his mother's insurance office, which was located across the street. He was also carrying a garbage bag. There were a dozen or so cans in the bottom. Apparently Mercy Woodyard saved aluminum cans for Lovie.

"Lee and I can fill this one up," he said.

"I don't need help!" Lovie's cracked voice was loud.

"I know you don't," Joe said, "but we need the exercise."

The old woman couldn't physically stop us from picking up the beer and soda cans that were scattered all over the sidewalk. But she would have if she could have. She muttered, "Smarty-pants kids. Think I can't take care of myself!" and similar remarks. Once or twice she yelled, "Don't mess with me! Just let me alone!" Our efforts were not being appreciated.

But at last the sidewalk was clear, and Joe knotted the top of the sack he and I had filled, then swung it into the back of her truck. Lovie tossed in the second sack herself. As she stood beside Joe, I was surprised to see that she was just a couple of inches shorter than he was. Which made her about my height, since I'm just under six feet and Joe's a bit over.

She stepped up on the curb, still glaring at us. "I s'pose you want thanks," she said. Her dark eyes, peering out from under the formerly white hat, snapped angrily.

"They're not notorious," I said. "I mean, necessary! There's no need to thank us."

"Well, I won't!" The old woman leaned closer to me. I tried not to shrink away. "You're that TenHuis girl, aren't you?"

"My mother was Sally TenHuis," I said. "My name is Lee McKinney."

She giggled. It had a wicked sound. Then she pointed at Joe. "All the TenHuis girls — they like 'em tall and dark!" She climbed into the old truck, still giggling maniacally. Before she closed the door she leaned out and spoke once more. "Tall and dark! Tall and dark! That's the way those TenHuis girls like 'em!"

Joe grabbed my arm. "Come on," he said. He turned me toward the Sidewalk Café and our belated lunch.

"That old woman is spooky," I said.

"Yep," Joe said. He grinned and slid his arm around me. "How do you think your mom would have liked having *her* for a mother-in-law?"

CHAPTER 4

I whirled to look at Joe, stepped on a piece of ice, and nearly fell flat on the sidewalk.

Joe grabbed my arm and kept me upright. "Whoops!" he said. "Are you okay?"

"No! I'm shocked beyond words! Are you telling me that old crazy Lovie is the mother of the guy my mom almost married?"

Joe looked down, shuffled his feet, and *um*ed and *er*ed the way men do when they realize they've put a foot into it up to the hip joint. "Well, uh, I thought Aunt Nettie told you last night."

"No! She told me about Bill Dykstra. And she told me his mother was still here in Warner Pier. But she dodged away from telling me who his mother was. I was going to ask *you* about her. Aunt Nettie said I wouldn't have any reason to know her."

"What? Everybody knows Lovie Dykstra."

"I know Lovie by sight, of course, but I didn't know her last name. Besides, Aunt

41

Nettie called her by a different first name. Vita."

"I've never heard her called that." Joe gestured toward the Sidewalk Café. "Come on. Let's get some lunch."

"I can't eat a bite. I'll just go back to the office." Then I stamped my boot. "No! I can't do that! I can't let Aunt Nettie see how upset I am!"

Joe looked at me closely. "You're not going to cry, are you?"

"No!" I denied it, but the tears were already oozing over my lids and down my cheeks.

Joe looked so woeful I thought he was going to hug me, right there at Fifth Avenue and Peach Street, a public display of affection that would be most unlike him. But he merely turned me around. "Come on," he said. "We'll go up to my place."

I didn't argue. I followed him across the street to a door between an antique store and a dress shop, both closed for the winter. He opened the door, and led me up the narrow steps to the apartment we were planning to share in three months. He waited until we were inside before he hugged me.

"I'm sorry, Lee. First, I thought you knew Lovie was Bill Dykstra's mother. Second, I didn't realize how shocked you'd be by the news. Lovie's such a joke around Warner Pier . . ."

"That's what upsets me, Joe! Last night I learned that my mother jilted her high school sweetheart practically at the door of the church. Then he committed suicide! Aunt Nettie told me his mother had been a science teacher. Now I learn that she's become so eccentric that she's a joke to everyone in town! She must have gone completely insane! Was this all my mother's fault?"

"Don't be silly! Mental illness — bipolar disorder or schizophrenia or depression or whatever was wrong with Billy and with his mother — is not caused by being jilted! Or by the suicide of a son. It has a physical cause. Your mother wasn't to blame for Bill and Lovie having some sort of chemical imbalance."

"I guess not. But it's so sad!"

Joe helped me out of my coat, seated me on his couch, and put his arms around me again. "It *is* an unhappy story," he said. "Lovie has become such an object of derision around here that I forgot that she has a tragic past. I'm sorry I was callous, Lee. Thanks for reminding me that her life is truly sad."

I laid my head on Joe's shoulder and cried

silently for a few minutes. He was smart enough not to say anything until I sat up and blew my nose.

"I guess you're still not in the mood for lunch at the Sidewalk," he said. "I can make us a grilled cheese sandwich."

"Sounds great. If you'll do that, I'll try to do something about my face."

I went into Joe's bathroom, washed my face with cold water, and repaired what damage I could. Thank goodness I gave up wearing elaborate makeup when I left Dallas and my earlier career as a trophy wife. If I'd had to contour three shades of eye shadow, I think I would have started crying again. But I managed to keep my eyes dry while I redid the minimal makeup I wear these days, and I had brushed my hair and put it back into its George Washington–style queue by the time I joined Joe in the kitchen.

He'd made six grilled cheese sandwiches and heated up at least a quart of cream of tomato soup.

"Why so much food?" I said. "Are you opening your own café?"

"No, but I did something nervy. I called Mom and asked her to come up and have lunch with us. Do you mind?"

"Why should I mind? I like your mom."

"I asked her because she knows as much about Lovie as anybody in Warner Pier does, and I thought you might have some more questions."

"As long as we don't have to argue about the reception."

"I'll try to head her off."

A few minutes later, Mercy Woodyard came up from her insurance office, just a few doors down the street. As usual, she looked as if she were posing for a fashion spread on what a successful career woman should wear. The black flannel double-breasted coat — full-length — topped a gray pantsuit that could have stepped right out of *Vogue* or *Elle*. She had a sterling silver pin on her lapel and wore a string of pearls I was willing to bet had not come from Wal-Mart. The shine on her dressy black boots made me hide my feet under my chair, and her makeup was perfect.

The only thing I could top her with was my hair. Thanks to the DNA I pulled out of the TenHuis gene pool, I'm a natural blonde; Mercy gets her tasteful shade though regular appointments with a good hairstylist.

Mercy always made me feel unkempt, but I reminded myself that she was not really suitably dressed for Warner Pier. A businesswoman shouldn't outclass her customers, and Warner Pier is a resort town whose usual wear is divided between khaki and denim. A more casual style would be better for Mercy's situation, I thought, though my flannel-lined jeans, turtleneck, and scuffed boots might be erring in the other direction.

Mercy, who owns Warner Pier's only insurance agency, is very likely the most successful businesswoman in Warner Pier. I guess she figures she might as well look like it. But Mercy is also a nice person, and she seemed to like me. Plus, she was busy with her own affairs and usually didn't show signs of wanting to run Joe's life or mine. That's quite a set of advantages in a future mother-in-law.

The wedding reception was the first bone of contention we'd run into, and I was determined to stand firm on that.

We sat at the kitchen table, and I told Mercy that Joe and I were going into Holland that week to pick out dishes and silver.

"I've had people ask about our selections," I said, "so I guess we should do it, even though I'm embarrassed about the whole thing, since we've both been married before."

"Of course you should do it," Mercy said,

tapping a finger on one of Joe's plastic plates. "It's not as if you don't need those things. And it's not as if anybody in Warner Pier gave either of you a present the first time around. Besides, people don't have to buy a wedding gift unless they want to.

"Which reminds me, somebody told me about a band that sounds great. They play oldies — for my generation — and new stuff, too. They're out of Ann Arbor, and they're called the Neocrats."

"We decided not to have a band," Joe said.

"Oh, I know. But I could handle it — it wouldn't be much. And I'd love to do it for you."

"No, Mercy," I said.

Then Joe cut in. "Forget the band, Mom. I told Lee that you could tell her about Lovie."

"What about Lovie? I saw you two helping her with her cans. And I could see that she was swearing at you over it."

"I was being selfish," I said. "I wanted all those cans off our sidewalk." Then I took a deep breath and plunged in. "Mercy, Warner Pier merchants are so — well, snotty — about anything that might ruin the appearance of the town. You have to paint buildings certain colors. You have to have signs of a certain style and size. But poor old

Lovie has that awful junk business — unpainted and trashy — and nobody ever says a word. Is it just because people feel sorry for her?"

"I assure you it's not! In fact, there have been several attempts to get Lovie's Recycling Center closed down."

Joe cleared his throat. "It was one of the first things I had to research after I became city attorney," he said. "She's grandfathered in. She had the shop there on the highway before that area was annexed to the city, so they can't get rid of her."

"Even with all that junk and trash?"

"As long as she keeps it indoors or behind that high fence, she's legal. Sentiment has nothing to do with it." Joe turned to his mother. "Until an hour ago I didn't realize that Lee didn't know about Lovie's connection with the guy her mom almost married."

I felt tears welling again. "That was awful."

"Yes, Lee, it was tragic. But it has nothing to do with you. And there's more to Lovie's story than her son's suicide."

"Joe says you know a lot about her."

"As much as anybody, probably. Her husband died shortly after I began working at the insurance agency. Joe was just a baby. We had to settle her insurance claim, get all the legal records together." She looked at me sharply. "There's no secret about any of this. I mean, if you have any questions, I wouldn't be giving out any confidential information."

"For one thing," I said, "what's her name? Aunt Nettie said her name was Vita. But Joe says he's never heard of her being called anything but Lovie."

"Her name is Lovita. Before her husband died, most people called her Vita. But he always called her Lovie. A pet name, I guess. After he died, she began to identify herself as Lovie Dykstra, and it caught on."

"Does she have any relatives?"

"Not that I know of. She had that older son, Ed, the one who went to Canada. So far as I know, he never came back, even after the draft dodgers who took asylum in Canada were pardoned. He might still be alive."

"There are so many Dykstras around here . . ."

"Yes, but they'd be only second or third cousins of Lovie's husband, if they are related at all. I'm under the impression that she avoids them. Lovie was originally from Wisconsin. If she has any relatives, they'd be over there."

Mercy sipped her cup of tomato soup.

"You young things won't believe it, but Lovie was a real stunner when she taught me high school science. A beautiful woman. And a talented teacher."

When Lovita Dykstra — then a newlywed — moved to Warner Pier, Mercy explained, she had been tall and slim, with dramatic dark eyes and hair. She and her husband, Edward, had lived quietly, and their two little boys were four years apart. When the boys were still small, Lovita had commuted to Western Michigan University, in Kalamazoo, to get her degree and teacher's certification. Then she'd landed a job as a science teacher in Warner Pier.

"She developed a great science program," Mercy said. "She focused on ecology before the rest of us even knew what the word meant. She was — well, nuts isn't too strong a word — she was nuts on the environment."

Apparently her older son, Ed, had followed in her ecological footsteps. "Ed was a class ahead of me at Warner Pier High," Mercy said. "He was a straight arrow in high school, but he went off the track in college."

Ed had been an Eagle Scout and a camp counselor, leading all sorts of groups and training programs to get young people to understand and protect the natural environment, she said. That had apparently led him into trouble.

"This was the late sixties, early seventies, remember," Mercy said. "There was still a lot of demonstrating going on. Ed joined a group that was protesting about the environment. Then he moved into the antiwar movement. He grew the required mat of hair and reportedly smoked a lot of pot. The gossip was that he lived in a *commune.* We all knew what that meant. Or thought we did."

At one time, Mercy said, Lovita had said she blamed herself for involving Ed in her own concerns for the environment, concerns that had eventually led him to the antiwar movement and his subsequent flight to Canada.

And Lovie's husband, Ed Sr., had not been sympathetic to Ed's actions.

"I think it caused a major split in the family," Mercy said. "Though Lovie and Ed Sr. never separated."

"It's not as if her son was a career criminal," I said.

Mercy gave a "what can you do?" shrug. "A lot of things happened to Lovie. First, Ed Jr. was a big disappointment to her husband. Second, because of Ed's problems

51

and her participation in demonstrations, the board of education became suspicious of her teaching. She had to fight not to be fired. Third, Bill committed suicide. Fourth, her husband began to have poor health. He was in and out of the hospital a dozen times with heart problems before he died. That was five years or so after Bill's suicide."

"How awful!"

"I guess Ed Sr.'s death was the last straw for Lovie. She took her retirement in a lump sum, bought that junkyard out on the highway, and renamed it Lovie's Recycling Center. It's not a real recycling center, of course. She doesn't have any equipment beyond a can crusher. She just collects stuff and hauls it into Holland."

Mercy reached over and patted my hand. "Anyway, Lee, she had a lot of problems. But people have had more problems than she did and kept on with life without becoming the town eccentric. If she's — well, cracked — I doubt that your mother had anything to do with her becoming that way."

I nodded. "I guess that's not what's bothering me, really. The problem is, my mom has always refused to come back to Warner Pier. But I wanted — we wanted her to come to our wedding. So I called and more or less twisted her arm like a pretzel until she said she'd come."

"But she did say she'd come?"

"Yes! Now I wonder — should I have insisted? Is my mom so despised around Warner Pier that it — won't be a happy experience for her?"

Mercy smiled. "I don't think the villagers will grab their pitchforks and form mobs, Lee."

"Oh, I know. But I wonder if she knows what's happened to Lovie. I guess I'd better warn her."

"That might be tactful. But it shouldn't stop her from coming."

"And the other thing is, why did she ask Aunt Nettie about this old sheriff?"

"Which old sheriff?"

"I don't remember. It was one of those Dutch names."

I expected that remark to get a laugh out of Mercy. It seems as if at least half of the natives of western Michigan are descendants of Dutch settlers. Tall blonds are everywhere, and our telephone directories have more 'Van' names than they do Smiths. I thought my reference would be considered a joke.

Instead Mercy got a look of real horror. "Not Van Hoosier? Carl Van Hoosier?"

"I think that was it."

Mercy leaned closer to me and gripped my hand until I thought my fingers would drop off. "Stay away from him!" she said. "Whatever you do, don't get mixed up with Carl Van Hoosier!"

CHOCOLATE CHAT:
BIRTH OF AN OBSESSION

I apparently loved chocolate from the moment I was born and loved books from the moment I could sit in my mother's lap and be read to.

This must have been genetic; my mother loved both chocolate and reading, particularly reading mysteries.

She told me that as a very small child I called chocolate milk "choc." Once, she said, I asked for "choc," and she replied, "As soon as I finish my chapter."

I answered, "Whenever I ask for choc, you *always* say, 'As soon as I finish my chapter.' "

She helped set my priorities forever — mysteries and chocolate. But I'm not yet sure which order they come in.

— *JoAnna Carl*

CHAPTER 5

It was gratifying to see that Mercy's reaction had left Joe as surprised as I was.

"What's the deal on Van Hoosier?" he said. "Don't tell me that Warner County, that absolute bastion of virtue, once had a crooked sheriff."

"I'm sure every county in the United States has had one or two crooked sheriffs in its history," Mercy said. She'd released her grip on my hand and seemed to be trying to compose herself. "Van Hoosier never stood trial or anything. There was simply a lot of gossip about him."

"Aunt Nettie said she thought he was dead," I said.

But Mercy shook her head. "I don't think so. I think I would have heard about it." She stood up. "I've got to get back to work."

"Wait a minute, Mom," Joe said. "Just what was Van Hoosier accused of?"

"It was just gossip."

"What kind of gossip?"

Mercy sighed. "When I was in high school — just before your mom would have been in high school, Lee — the gossip was that if Van Hoosier caught a couple parked on a back road it was bad news. Supposedly he would handcuff the boy in the back of the patrol car, then . . ."

Her voice failed her, and Joe finished her sentence. "He'd rape the girl?"

Mercy nodded. "As I say, nobody ever got him into court. And since he was a county official, he wasn't over here by Lake Michigan too much. He usually hung out over near Dorinda — wouldn't get too far from the courthouse. So very few Warner Pier couples were involved. Or would admit it. Back then — well, girls were hesitant to report things like that."

She looked from Joe to me then, and her face was defiant. "But I believed the stories," she said.

"They could be true," Joe said. "However, the same story was going around when I was in high school, and we had a different sheriff by then. And the attack always happened to some couple that someone knew, but they'd never tell the name."

"You mean like an urban legend?"

Joe nodded, and Mercy went on. "I hope

56

that's all it was."

Her story seemed to cast a pall over the lunch table, and we were all morose as we rinsed the dishes and stuck them in the dishwasher. I was the one who broke the silence. "I guess I could find out if Van Hoosier's still alive," I said.

Mercy's reaction was almost identical to the one Aunt Nettie had displayed fourteen hours earlier, when I mentioned looking into Bill Dykstra's death. She snapped one word out. "No!"

I stared at her, and she went on. "No, Lee. That curiosity bug of yours is a symptom of your intelligence, and I don't like to discourage it, but this is not the time or the situation for curiosity. The situation with the Dykstras and your mother — it's over. People have nearly forgotten. Let it be!"

Then Mercy put on her dressy black coat, buttoned it up, and headed back to her office.

She left me feeling uneasy. How could she tell me not to be curious when there was so much to be curious about? It was like hearing a joke — not that this situation was funny — and missing the punch line.

Why had my mother run away from Warner Pier on her wedding day? Why had Bill Dykstra committed suicide? Why had his mother become the town's eccentric?

Or one of the town's eccentrics; we have plenty.

And where did this former sheriff fit in? Had my mom and her young fiancé been among his victims? I hated that thought so much that I stuffed it deep in the back of my brain.

Mercy and Aunt Nettie had both advised me not to try to find the answers to any of those questions. But they hadn't made me promise.

However, right at that moment I had to go back to work. Between having emotional storms and quizzing Mercy, I'd taken a long lunch hour. Aunt Nettie wouldn't jump on me, but the shop was really busy and was likely to stay that way through Easter. I was having to take time off for wedding preparations anyway, so my tardiness made me feel guilty as I jaywalked back to TenHuis Chocolade.

And it turned out that I had reason to feel guilty. While I was at Joe's stuffing myself with grilled cheese and interrogating my future mother-in-law, TenHuis Chocolade had been hit by a crisis.

Dolly Jolly, our most striking employee, boomed out the news as I came in the door. "The jazz band bunnies didn't come!"

Dolly is even taller than I am and is twice as broad. Her hair is a bright red, and her face is dotted with matching red freckles. Her voice is just naturally loud. Every word she speaks seems to be coming through a powerful speaker system. She's also a brilliant cook. She had joined TenHuis Chocolade six months earlier and was rapidly becoming Aunt Nettie's right-hand helper.

"I thought the bunnies were in the UPS delivery yesterday!" she said. "But they weren't!"

"Have you checked with Ohio?"

"Not yet! We just now quit looking for the molds!" Dolly clutched her hands together. "We need to make and ship this afternoon!"

I slipped out of my jacket and reached for my Rolodex. The nation's largest supplier of molds for chocolatiers is in Ohio. We had placed a special order with them, asking for replicas of four molds originally made by T. C. Weygandt & Co. in the 1950s. Each mold showed a bunny playing a different jazz instrument — drum, banjo, accordion, saxophone. A Grand Rapids band instrument company had ordered two hundred of each to use as favors at a school music convention they were helping to sponsor.

The order for eight hundred six-inch rabbits wasn't going to make or break our profits for the year, of course, though it was a nice piece of business. The point was that we deliver our product as promised. The order hadn't been placed until late, so we had known we were cutting it close. In fact, Aunt Nettie hadn't wanted to accept the order. But when the Ohio people said they could ship the molds in ten days, Dolly talked her into it.

As Dolly said, we could "make and ship" the same day and, if we did, we could handle it. But we couldn't make the darn things until we had the molds.

It took five minutes for me to get the UPS tracking number from the Ohio mold shop. Then I went to the UPS site. Dolly was still standing beside me, looking almost tearful.

"They sent them second day," I said, "instead of overnight. But this says the molds are on the truck. At least the number indicates 'out for delivery.' I guess Leon will deliver them today."

Dolly's face became more anguished than ever. "But Leon won't be here until after four thirty!"

At our request, TenHuis Chocolade is the UPS man's final stop before he heads back to Holland. I knew he was probably someplace in Warner Pier at that moment, making earlier deliveries.

"I'll find him," I said.

As I've said, Warner Pier is a small town. We all know the UPS man's delivery schedule. I got on the phone and began to try to track him down.

Leon had been by the bank, I learned, and by the hardware store. The hardware store clerk, naturally, had been in high school with my mom, so she took the opportunity to quiz me about her. "Is she coming to the wedding?"

A day earlier I wouldn't have thought anything about her question. Now it infuriated me, but I tried to answer as if it were a normal question.

"She says she'll be here," I said. "Maybe I can catch Leon at the Garden Shop." I hung up, seething, and phoned the new number.

"He brought us a big shipment of bird-feeders," Tom Hilton, the Garden Shop owner, said. Then he added, "By the way, Lee, is your mother coming to your wedding?"

Again I had to force myself to make a casual answer. "Sure is, Tom. She's fleeing up. I mean, flying! She's flying in for the wedding."

"I'll look forward to seeing her. We graduated from high school the same year. You know, she kinda left Warner Pier with its jaw dragging."

I cut him off. "Tom, I'll talk to you later. I've got to run away — I mean run! I'm going to run to the corner and see if I can catch Leon at Shorewood Gifts." I hung up, mentally cursing my unruly tongue, and grabbed my jacket.

When I got to the corner and looked toward the river, to my relief I saw the big brown bulk of the UPS truck. Leon had left Shorewood Gifts and was just putting his foot into his truck. By yelling in a loud, unladylike manner and running down the street waving my arms, I managed to catch him. And he found the molds. I asked Leon to make us his final pickup stop of the day, as usual, so Dolly, Aunt Nettie, and the other hairnet ladies had two hours to get the jazz band bunnies ready to go. Luckily, they weren't to get a fancy wrapping.

Between that crisis and about a million phone calls, I was able to put my mother, Bill Dykstra, his mother, and Sheriff Van Hoosier out of my mind until quitting time. Then I thought the whole situation over. Despite the warnings from Aunt Nettie and from Mercy, I wanted to know more. But I didn't want to start a whole lot of talk by asking questions around town. So, how could I look into it? How could I figure out what had happened more than thirty years ago?

I decided to start at the Warner Pier Public Library. The library was open in the evenings for the convenience of students. Joe was tied up with a city planning meeting that night, so I was on my own.

I told Aunt Nettie I would work late and eat a sandwich when I got home. She left, apparently unsuspicious. I worked until six p.m. — nibbling on a couple of Mexican vanilla truffles ("light vanilla interior coated with milk chocolate," according to our sales sheets). Once I was convinced Aunt Nettie wasn't coming back, I locked the shop and headed for the library.

The Warner Pier Public Library, like a lot of our buildings, is a prize example of high Victorian architecture. It was, I understand, originally built to house the Methodist Church. Along in the 1950s the Methodists built a snazzy brick number out on the highway, apparently designed to attract summer visitors, and their old building with its gingerbread-trimmed steeple was sold to the city for use as a library. The county library system had to level the sloping sanctuary floor and to add an unsightly ramp for handicapped access, but much of the original Queen Anne Victorian is intact.

The clerk at the circulation desk directed me to the high school yearbooks. "Reference," she said. "Upstairs." I trotted up to what had once been the church balcony and was now the library's reference room. Shelves on one side of the room were packed with bound newspapers and copies of the *Watchman* yearbook of Warner Pier High School. Back near the door to the minuscule elevator was a microfilm reader. A couple of standard oak study tables, cabinets holding microfilm, and racks of encyclopedias and other reference works took up the rest of the space. The only people there were two high school girls who were sitting at one of the tables, giggling. At the sight of an adult they tried to act serious, but it was a losing battle.

I smiled at them and went straight to the yearbook shelf. It took only a moment for me to locate the right years, and I took the four yearbooks that covered my mother's high school career to the seat farthest from the two students. I started with the year my mother graduated, and within seconds I was looking at my mom's senior picture — dated hairstyle and all.

She had been blond — all the TenHuises are blond — her face round and pretty. Of course, the black-and-white picture didn't show how blue her eyes were, and the sophisticated travel agent that my mom had become would have been horrified by the pose, which featured hands clasped beside her left ear.

I stared at the picture, and I realized something surprising. I had never seen it before in my life.

In fact, the only pictures I had ever seen of my mom as a child or a teenager were displayed on Aunt Nettie's dresser. There was a family shot taken by a professional photographer and showing my grandparents seated side by side, with a teenaged Uncle Phil standing behind them and my mom sitting on her father's lap. She was missing her front teeth. There was an obviously posed snapshot of my mom at thirteen or fourteen roasting hot dogs on the beach with Uncle Phil, by then a young man. And that was it. Aunt Nettie might well have a box of photos tucked away in some closet, but she'd never dug them out to show me. And I'd never asked her to do that.

I'd already concluded that my mom had deliberately turned her back on Warner Pier when she ran away. Now I realized that if she had taken any pictures or mementos when she began a new life in Texas, she'd never shared them with me. Until I came to

Warner Pier I had never seen a picture of her made before she and my dad were married.

I'd never seen her high school graduation picture. The thought really amazed me.

I turned to the yearbook index and tracked down all the other mentions of my mother for her senior year. She'd been a member of mixed chorus and girls' sextet and was pictured with the choir — one of twenty-five girls wearing the same unbelievably unbecoming dress. I couldn't believe Mom had ever been that plump. She'd been secretary of the Future Homemakers of America. To my surprise, I discovered she'd been a member of the honor society. Mom had always told me she wasn't much of a student. I wondered why she'd refused to admit she had good grades.

By then I was to the final entry in the index. It turned out to be the page with pictures from the senior prom.

And there was Mom, wearing a short but dressy dress, with her hair twisted up onto the top of her head. And with her was a tall, raw-boned guy with dark hair, worn as long as the other boys'. I didn't need to read the caption. It had to be Bill Dykstra.

"Tall and dark," Lovie had said. "That's

66

the way those TenHuis girls like 'em. Tall and dark."

I studied the picture and decided she must be right. Tall and dark Bill was the same general physical type as my tall and dark dad. Bill was also the same general type as Joe. But Rich, my first husband, had been shorter and fairer. Maybe that's why our marriage was such a flop, I thought wryly.

I put that idea aside and looked at the yearbooks from other years my mom would have been a student at WPHS. The books were more of the same, of course. Two years earlier I found Bill's senior picture. It showed a long-haired kid; he'd matured physically in the two years between his senior year and my mom's senior prom. He'd been on the basketball team, I noted, and on the stage crew for the senior play. He'd been vice president of the Ecology Club; had his mother influenced him? He had also made the honor society. I wondered why he had gone to trade school, rather than college.

He and my mom were also pictured together at the senior prom the year Bill had graduated. But that year, instead of the formal portraits of couples used in my mom's senior year, the prom page had been a collage of snapshots.

In the one of Mom and Bill, both were laughing. I stared at Bill's face. He had his arm around Mom. She was looking up at him admiringly. He was grinning from ear to ear. He looked completely happy.

He certainly didn't look as if he would turn suicidal just two years later.

Someone cleared his throat behind me, and I jumped all over. I looked up to see one of the city councilmen, Raleigh "Rollie" Taylor.

"Sorry," said Rollie. "I didn't mean to startle you, Lee. Are you researching wedding etiquette?"

I slammed the yearbook shut. "Not tonight, Rollie."

"I wanted to make sure you knew that if Oprah Winfrey married Deepak Chopra, she'd be Oprah Chopra."

I chuckled. "I can always count on you to keep me up on these things."

Rollie is the classic jolly fat man. I'd been horrified when I first heard his cruel nickname. But when a boy whose name is Raleigh grows up to weigh a hundred pounds more than he should and to be the town's most enthusiastic teller of jokes, I guess it's inevitable that his nickname will be Rollie. At least his friends hadn't added "Poly" after it.

And Rollie did have friends. This had been demonstrated at the latest city election, when he ran for Warner Pier City Council in a hotly contested race and handily beat a more svelte candidate.

Rollie had taught social studies at Warner Pier High School for thirty years. Joe had been one of his students. Now, as city attorney, Joe worked with Rollie. They frequently sparred during the meetings, mostly about money. Rollie had a reputation for being tightfisted with his own money — with the occasional splurge on travel abroad — and he definitely was tight with the city's money. That's a good thing in general, I guess, but a few months earlier Joe had thought Rollie was urging the council to cut a few legal and financial corners on a case involving an injured city employee, and they'd disagreed publicly.

Joe had won the council's support, and Rollie's proposal had been voted down. Rollie smiled his usual smile, even though he'd lost the vote and might have been expected to be unhappy. Then he said, "It's okay. Joe and I have been buddies since Lansing."

Lansing? Lansing is the capital of Michigan and home of Michigan State University. But Joe had gone to the University of Michigan, in Ann Arbor. I didn't understand the reference. But since that time Rollie had repeatedly twitted Joe with references to Lansing. I didn't get the joke, and Joe hadn't reacted to it. I hadn't asked Joe to explain.

But Joe didn't seem to dislike Rollie. Nobody did. He belonged to every committee and club in town. If we'd held a popularity contest, Rollie would have come in near the top, even if he never did buy a round at the postcouncil bull sessions in the bar of the Sidewalk Café.

Rollie reached over and picked up the yearbook I had just slammed shut. "That was the first year I taught at WP High," he said. He thumbed through the faculty section and pointed to his picture. "I can't believe I ever had that much hair."

"Everybody had a lot of hair then. You were right in style." Rollie's hair had been thick and dark then, and it had probably been pushing the rules about length for teachers. Now his hair was gray and cut much shorter. It was also thinner on top, though I wouldn't have called Rollie bald. The main difference between Rollie of thirty-plus years earlier and today was about fifty pounds. He'd been plump then, but he was obese now.

Rollie closed the book and asked the question I'd grown used to. "Is your mother coming for your wedding?"

I tried to answer casually. "That's the plan."

"Great!" Rollie leaned toward me and dropped his voice almost to a whisper.

"Lee, your mom was such a sweet girl. Why has she never come back to Warner Pier?"

"She came back for Uncle Phil's funeral."

"That was a mighty quick trip." He frowned. "She's not still worried about Bill Dykstra, is she?"

"I really don't know, Rollie. She's never expelled — I mean, explained! She's never explained why she doesn't want to come back."

He stood up and leaned closer to me. "When she comes, be sure she talks to me."

"Why?" My voice was sharp, even to my own ears.

"Bill was a troubled young man," Rollie said. "I might know some things about him that would come as a surprise — even to Sally."

CHAPTER 6

I stared at him for a moment. And suddenly I was mad. Just where did he get off wanting to tell my mom things "even she might not know" about Bill Dykstra? What she knew or didn't know wasn't any of Rollie's business.

And it wasn't any of my business, either. My mom hadn't asked me to snoop around in her past. She would probably resent my doing so. And she'd be sure to resent a former high school teacher — a person she had never even mentioned knowing — snooping around in her life.

"Listen, Rollie," I said. "I think you would be wise to drop this."

"Why?"

"Because my mom has never talked about why she left Warner Pier. She has put the whole town behind her."

"That may be significant in itself, Lee."

"Yes, it may. Or it may not. I don't know

about that. But I do know one thing. I know Mom hasn't spent the past thirty-three years mooning around over her high school sweetheart and his tragic death. She moved on. She married my dad — he's a nice guy, and for at least fifteen years they were happy. When their marriage broke up, she moved on again. She found a job she liked and developed it into a successful career. She raised a daughter — and she was a highly supportive mother. She has friends, she has a good job, she owns a nice home, she travels all over the world, and she seems to enjoy herself thoroughly."

I stood up and gathered the old yearbooks into a pile. "I suggest that you and I follow her lead and forget the past."

Rollie smiled his jolly smile. The one that turned his eyes into little slits. "Of course, you're right, Lee. Time wounds all heels."

He didn't explain what he meant by that. What heels? I decided not to ask.

Rollie turned away, humming softly, and went to the shelf of encyclopedias. He pulled out the first volume and took it to a table. By the time I had the yearbooks back on the shelf he was immersed in the book, but he looked up and smiled at me as I left.

I'd just bawled Rollie out. Why was he smiling?

I left the library feeling righteous. I was nearly home before I began to regret one thing.

I hadn't looked Sheriff Carl Van Hoosier up in the library's newspaper files before Rollie confronted me. Now I couldn't. My outburst had ruined any excuse I had for looking into what had happened.

That thought made me feel guilty and caused me to give myself another lecture on staying out of my mother's business. At the same time, I admitted to myself that I wasn't exactly sure that everything I'd told Rollie about her was true.

Those facts were one way to look at my mother's life. She *had* moved on after Bill Dykstra's suicide. She *had* married a nice guy, she *had* built a successful career, she *did* own a nice home and travel the world.

But there was another way of looking at it. She had married my dad without realizing that her husband was not ambitious and that he would be happy to stay in his hometown forever; she had always felt that she was stuck in Prairie Creek. And neither of my parents had any financial sense. I used to lie in bed at night and listen to them argue about money. My stepmother had finally straightened my dad's finances out, but my mom was still up to her eyebrows in credit card debt, mainly because of her travel habit — even travel agents don't get everything free. Her "nice" home was a dinky condo she had never decorated because she didn't have the money. And, yes, she did have friends, but she'd never dated anyone seriously since she divorced my dad. In fact, I knew of a couple of nice guys she'd deliberately dropped when they seemed to be getting serious.

I'd told Rollie that she had been a "supportive" mother. That was true. Of course, she hadn't always supported me in the direction I wanted to go. When I was in my late teens, I'd felt pushed and prodded to do things — such as beauty pageants — that Mom had wanted me to do. I'd been enrolled in classes she couldn't afford — speech lessons, musical training, exercise classes, even "charm school" — not because those things represented what I wanted to do, but because Mom felt they'd help me "get ahead." Getting ahead by developing my brains and professional skills hadn't seemed to be an option. Let's face it; she hadn't believed I was smart enough to develop professional skills. She thought I'd have to rely on my looks, so I'd better make the most of them.

Despite their other differences, my dad

had supported her plans for me. My dad is a Texan. Texans like their daughters to be admired for their beauty and pretty ways. He had bragged about his daughter the beauty queen, but it wouldn't have occurred to him to brag about his daughter the A student. I made the honor roll, but I wasn't encouraged to admit it. My mother thought it was just luck, and it simply wasn't important to my dad.

For five years I'd tried to please them, entering pageant after pageant. Then I made the disastrous decision to marry Rich Gottrocks — I mean, Godfrey — only to find out that he was disappointed, maybe even angry, when he learned there were a few brains under my natural blond hair. It doesn't do your ego much good when your husband is disappointed because you earned a four-point grade average.

When I got married both my parents had given sighs of relief. Their little girl (all five foot eleven-plus inches of her) had married a wealthy man who would take care of her. They'd both thought I was crazy when I ditched the jewelry, the nice car, and the fancy house — along with Rich. And they thought I was crazier when I refused any financial settlement from him and even left the household goods behind.

But I couldn't blame my mother for my bad marriage. She'd approved — heck, even my dad had approved, though he and Rich had nothing in common. But I'd picked Rich out all on my own. I had only myself to blame.

I didn't yet understand why my mom had pushed me into the beauty pageant circuit, no matter how hard I dragged my heels. I didn't understand the upbringing she had had, the factors that had made her financially improvident and wild to travel the world whether she could afford to or not. I didn't understand why she'd never talked about her family much, why she'd never even mentioned having a fiancé who committed suicide.

And I didn't understand why she'd asked Aunt Nettie if Sheriff Carl Van Hoosier was still alive. I sure did wish that I'd researched Sheriff Van Hoosier before I committed myself to staying out of my mother's life.

But for nearly a week I stuck to that plan. I stayed out of my mom's life. And I would have stayed out forever, I guess, if Lovie hadn't intervened.

It was a quiet Tuesday afternoon, and I was sitting at my computer in my glass cubicle, balancing the TenHuis Chocolade bank statement, when the bell on the street door tinkled. I looked up to see Lovie Dykstra — white hat, red pom-pom and all — coming in. She looked around the shop, glaring, fixed her eye on me, and started across the shop, headed for my office.

I didn't know why Lovie had come in, but I knew I didn't want her in my office. She'd be lots harder to get rid of if she came in there and sat down than if she simply stood at the counter. So I jumped to my feet and headed her off. I got into the shop before she could get past the counter and put her foot on my office threshold.

But I tried to be polite, even friendly. "Hello, Mrs. Dykstra. Let me offer you a sample of TenHuis chocolate."

She scowled. "I didn't come for candy. I came for information."

"You can have both." I went behind the sales counter and gestured at the chocolates in the glass cases. "Do you like light, dark, or white chocolate?"

"No. Your mother Sally TenHuis?"

"Yes. Why do you ask?"

Her scowl deepened into a glare. "What became of that girl?"

What interest did Lovie have in my mother? I'd been in Warner Pier nearly three years; why had the subject of my mother come up now? I decided I couldn't hand out information about my mother to a woman who might be unbalanced.

I gave a noncommittal answer. "My mom's doing fine. Why do you want to know?"

"Where is she?"

"Mrs. Dykstra, I'm not going to tell you anything about my mother until I understand why you want to know."

We stared at each other over the chocolates for a few moments. Then Lovie gave her cackling laugh. "Heh, heh, heh! I'll just ask *you* then."

"Ask me what?"

"How old are you, girl?"

It was the last question I'd expected. I'm sure my jaw gaped. "How old am I?"

"I guess you know!"

I decided I might as well tell her. "I'll be thirty next month. Why do you want to know?"

Lovie seemed to grow even angrier. She glared at me for another moment. Then her eyes took on a crafty look. "I guess you're like all these pretty women. You take a couple of years off."

I was getting as mad as she seemed to be. I turned abruptly, went into my office, and pulled my purse from my desk drawer. I snatched my driver's license out of my billfold, took it back to the counter, and stuck it under Lovie's nose. "You can check the birth date," I said.

Lovie read it, squinting at the small print and looking from the license to me and back again, almost as if she were checking to make sure I was really Susanna Lee McKinney, blond hair, hazel eyes, five feet eleven inches tall. And as she read it, her face seemed to crumple. She aged right before my eyes.

"That man always was a liar," she said.

"Who?"

Lovie glared at the floor and mumbled.

I was extremely puzzled. "What is it that you want?"

She mumbled again and turned toward the outside door. Suddenly I felt terribly sorry for her. But I couldn't imagine what I could do that would make her feel better. Desperate, I offered chocolate.

"Mrs. Dykstra, everyone who comes into TenHuis Chocolade gets a sample bonbon or truffle. Please let me give you one."

She looked back at me and spoke softly. "I just keep hoping."

"Hoping for what?" She didn't answer, but I ignored that. I escorted her to one of the two chairs we keep in the retail area. "Here, sit down a minute. And do let me get you some chocolate."

She let me put her in the chair, and she looked up at me almost as if she was pleading for something. But what?

I tried to smile. "Chocolate is full of theobromine. It actually does make you feel better when you're upset. Please have a piece."

"Flavanols," Lovie said. "They lower your blood pressure."

I was amazed. Was this some weird throwback to the days when Lovie had been a science teacher? "Right," I said. "Chocolate is *good* for you. It does contain flavanols. Do you like milk chocolate or dark chocolate?"

"Coffee?"

"Coffee flavored? Sure." I went to the counter and took out two chocolates — a mocha pyramid bonbon (described in our sales material as a "milky coffee-flavored interior in a dark chocolate pyramid") and a coffee truffle ("an all–milk chocolate truffle flavored with Caribbean coffee").

"Do you want to eat them now?" I asked. "Or take them with you?"

"Take 'em along."

I put the chocolates in a tiny box and tied it with a blue TenHuis bow. Then I brought it out from behind the counter and presented it to Lovie. As I held it out, she grasped my wrist.

81

My heart pounded. Was I in the clutches of a crazy woman? I resisted the impulse to pull away.

"Listen!" Lovie said. "I wouldn't bother your mother. She was a sweet young girl. I wanted to love her. I just need to know why she ran away in the first place."

"She's never talked to me about it, Mrs. Dykstra."

She let go of my arm. "I would never bother her. I just don't understand why that sheriff lied to me. Oh, he was an awful liar, I know. But why did he lie to me about Sally?"

She got to her feet and shuffled toward the door. As she opened it she seemed to become aware of the box in her hand. She turned and looked at me. She no longer looked angry.

"Thank you very much for the kind gift, Miss McKinney," she said. Her voice had lost its raspy quality. She sounded like a perfect lady.

"You are quite welcome," I replied.

After she left I stood there, blinking back tears.

What had all that been about? Why had Lovie come? Why had she wanted to know about my mom? Why had she wanted to know my age? Then the answer hit me.

"Oh, lordy!" I said the words aloud. "She thought Mom ran away from Warner Pier because she was pregnant and her fiancé was dead. She thought her son might have been my father. She thought she might be my grandmother."

I didn't know whether I should laugh or cry. I felt desperately sorry for Lovie. I almost felt sorry that my birth date had disappointed her.

But my mom had left Warner Pier two years before she married my dad. And I hadn't been born for eighteen months after their wedding.

At least the date was long enough after Mom left Warner Pier to be convincing. She might have been able to fake my age by six months or so, but a three-and-a-half-year difference was out of the question. No, my dad is really J. B. McKinney, of Prairie Creek, Texas. And Lovie is not my grandmother.

At least I knew how I felt about that. Relieved.

But Lovie had said "that sheriff" had lied to her. She must have been referring to the notorious Sheriff Carl Van Hoosier. He had apparently told her my mom left Prairie Creek for the traditional reason small-town girls left home thirty years ago.

I supposed that was possible, but I doubted it. My mom wasn't fanatically either prochoice or prolife, but I didn't think she would have had an abortion. And she couldn't have started airline school that next fall if she were carrying a baby, even one she gave up for adoption. Or I didn't think she could have.

But how did Sheriff Van Hoosier get into the act, anyway?

That night I talked to Aunt Nettie about the situation, and she was as confused as I was. I continued to think about the sheriff's lie from every angle for twenty-four hours, but it still didn't make sense. How could the ex-sheriff — crooked or not — fit into a picture that included Bill Dykstra's suicide and my mom fleeing from Warner Pier?

Even after my run-in with Lovie and my twenty-four hours of thinking, I might have stayed out of my mom's past if it hadn't been for the Way Back When column of the *Warner Pier Gazette*.

Most small-town newspapers, and even a few big-city ones, have that column. Some poor reporter is assigned to look at the microfilm of the newspaper from a hundred years earlier and to select a few items to edify the modern reader. In the *Gazette*'s case, they pick items not only from 100 years ago, but also from 150, from 50, and from 25. I never miss the column. You never know what it will disclose: the date some local building came to be constructed, a tell-all about the "pound the preacher" party given by members of the Methodist church in the early 1900s, or an insight into some other Michigan custom from the past. Once it had even described the up-to-the-minute service station and garage being built by a young World War II veteran, Henry Ten-Huis, who some years later became my grandfather.

This particular week, the 150-years-ago bit was a tirade on some forgotten politician, the 100 years ago described a big fire at the fruit basket factory, and the 50 years ago told about a big snow storm. It was the 25-years-ago item that caught my eye.

"Kemper Swartz is appointed Warner County Sheriff," it read. "He was selected to complete the term of Carl Van Hoosier, who resigned amid accusations of malfeasance in office."

So Van Hoosier's misdeeds had eventually caught up with him — eight years after my mom ran away from Warner Pier and her fiancé committed suicide.

But Joe's mom had said that Van Hoosier was never actually charged with anything.

She could be right. "Accusations," the Way Back When column said. Not "convictions." Maybe Van Hoosier had dodged the bullet, had avoided charges. Maybe the case against him wasn't strong enough.

I studied that last phase. "Malfeasance in office." What did that mean, anyway?

Suddenly, I simply had to know. No matter what I'd told Rollie Taylor, I was going to find out more about Sheriff Carl Van Hoosier and what he had been up to twenty-five years earlier. And eight years before that.

CHAPTER 7

The first thing I did was call Chuck O'Riley, editor of the *Warner Pier Gazette.* The *Gazette* concentrates strictly on Warner Pier events and people, leaving the main county news to the *Dorinda Daily News,* published in our county seat.

It's always struck me as odd that almost nobody in Warner Pier subscribes to the *Dorinda Daily News.* You'd think we'd want to keep up on our county. But the Lake Michigan shore communities are so focused on the lake, art colonies, and tourism that we don't seem to be part of Warner County. If Warner Pier people read a newspaper other than the *Gazette,* it's likely to come from Holland, Grand Rapids, or Chicago.

The *Dorinda Daily News* owns the *Gazette,* so the *News* publisher is Chuck's boss. I'd found out earlier that Chuck has his own collection of archives, if you can call loose clippings in manila file folders archives. But he does have some microfilm.

Chuck told me to come by his office around three and he'd help me dig through the *Gazette* files. I was right on time. Chuck set me up with his microfilm reader, and I found the story that had inspired the item in the twenty-five-years-ago category.

It added very little to what the Way Back When column said. The headline might as well have been "Old Boys' Network Lets Sheriff Escape Justice."

The county commissioners had had an agenda item on unspecified charges against Sheriff Carl Van Hoosier. When the item came up, the head commissioner opened the discussion by announcing that Van Hoosier had tendered his resignation. The person making the charges, identified only as a county official, had agreed to let the matter drop. No hint of what the charges had been appeared in the *Warner Pier Gazette*. And Chuck assured me the *Gazette* story was the same one that had run in the *News*.

Only one phrase hinted at what Van Hoosier's sins had been. "I'm just an old-fashioned lawman," the sheriff said. "I'm not a bookkeeper. So I guess it's time for me to hand in my badge. Today's law enforcement is all paperwork and very little catching of criminals."

Sure.

The commissioners named Van Hoosier's chief deputy as acting sheriff, and the whole matter was swept under the rug without leaving a single lump. A check of commissioners' meetings for a month before the resignation and a month afterward didn't find any mention of the sheriff's office at all.

I left the microfilm viewer and stuck my head into Chuck's office. "Hey," I said. "Have you got a file on the sheriff himself? Carl Van Hoosier?"

"Nope," Chuck said. "I already checked. I never heard of the guy until that item showed up in the Way Back When."

Chuck is as broad as he is tall, with dark eyes that seem to be soaking up everything around him.

"Every *Gazette* editor has had his own system for keeping files — or not keeping them," he said. "Van Hoosier was long before my time. It would be pure luck if we had anything on him."

"Rats! I can't even find out if he's dead or alive."

"Maybe I can help you there. The *News* has part of its archives online. Eventually they'll get the *Gazette* on the system, too.

But we can access the *News* obits back to the dawn of time."

Chuck turned to his computer and called up the files of his parent newspaper. It took him quite a while to go through the "Vans" in the obituaries, since this is western Michigan, but in about ten minutes he looked at me and gestured toward the screen. "There are a dozen Van Hoosiers, but Carl is not among them. I guess he's still alive."

"That's hard to believe. He'd be really old."

"Let me call up the *News* county government file. Maybe it has something about him."

Chuck gave the computer more commands, then stood up. "Here, Lee, you take a look."

I sat down in Chuck's place, looked the system over, and figured out where to type in the keywords. Before an hour was up I had found out quite a bit from old stories about county government.

Van Hoosier had been in office nearly fifteen years when my mom abruptly left home. He wasn't from our end of the county; he lived about thirty miles east of Warner Pier. There were no major complaints about him in the early 1970s, but one headline for a county commissioners meeting did read, "Citizens Complain about Lack of Patrols." The story said that lakeside property owners were unhappy because of erratic scheduling of patrols on Lake Shore Drive near the public access areas. The story didn't surprise me. That situation had still been a concern to Lake Shore Drive people when I worked for TenHuis Chocolade as a teenager. It was one of the reasons that Aunt Nettie's neighborhood voted to annex themselves to Warner Pier. Now the Warner Pier PD patrolled our area, and the situation was slightly better.

By the time Chuck started making noises about closing his office, I was strongly into research mode. So I grabbed a sandwich at the Sidewalk Café, moved my base of operations to the Warner Pier Public Library, and started on their microfilm. I didn't mess with the *Gazette.* I went to the *Dorinda Daily News* files. And I went straight to the year my mom had graduated from high school and run away from home. I started in January. The *News* issues of those days ran only eight to twelve pages, and I figured I could skip the classified pages, so I hoped to get through it by the time the library closed.

It was a momentous year. The Vietnam War was winding down, but antiwar demonstrations were still going on. Editorial columns looked at the events at Wounded Knee, *Roe v. Wade,* the end of the military draft, and the Equal Rights Amendment, which had just recently been OK'd by the U.S. Senate and sent on for the consideration of the state legislatures.

In local news, it was interesting to see what was written about the founding of TenHuis Chocolade. The story in the *Warner Pier Gazette* had been bigger, of course. Aunt Nettie had a framed copy of that one in our break room. But there had been a nice write-up in the *News,* on their once-a-week business page.

Warner Pier city government had barely been mentioned, but I did learn that Lindy's grandfather had been a city councilman in those days. And my grandfather had served on the park board. That explained why there was a Henry TenHuis Memorial Nature Trail in one of the parks that ran along the Warner River. I'd known it was there, but I'd never known what my grandfather did to deserve it. Apparently he laid the trail out.

Crime continued, both nationally and locally. In Warner Pier news, there was a lot of talk about drug sales, hippies, and attendant evils. Warner Pier had always depended on the tourist dollar; rowdy young counterculture types were not the sort of tourists the town liked. On the white-collar front, the cashier of the First National Bank of Dorinda was charged with embezzlement, and the records of the city clerk at Canton, a village north of Warner Pier, were found to be extremely irregular. There were no murders in the county that year, but several assault cases were filed. Most of the accused had Spanish surnames. I guess the hometown guys had been getting away with more than these newcomers were, thirty-three years ago.

The national crime front had been pretty interesting. There was a major robbery at a jewelry exchange in New York, and some inventive thief put up a false night deposit box outside a bank in Cleveland. At least a dozen merchants plunked their day's take inside before the thieves loaded the box into a stolen truck and carried it away.

That was also the year of the famous Quinn McKay kidnapping, in which the son of industrialist Benson McKay III was snatched in Chicago and held for ransom by a group that wanted money to fund their radical social agenda. He was released after several months by kidnappers he described as anonymous guys in ski masks. I'd read about the case in some historical article; the kidnappers had never been caught. We still heard about that around Warner Pier because the McKay family owned a cottage just south of Warner Pier. A Mrs. McKay — of the middle-aged-but-not-admitting-it type — came in for chocolate now and then. But not her stepson, Quinn McKay.

I couldn't help checking out the wedding stories, too, of course, since I had weddings on the brain. The most popular bridal gowns had Empire waistlines and puffy lace sleeves, like the one my mother had left behind. But the muslin dresses with cotton lace — the style she had worn when she married my dad — apparently didn't become fashionable until later.

The clothing ads showed teased hair and shirtdresses with A-line skirts that stopped just above the knee. The fabric stores had specials on polyester knits. Shoes had big clunky heels.

The *News* obituaries included my grandfather's, of course. And later a brief notice about the death of Bill Dykstra.

Sheriff Carl Van Hoosier didn't get a lot of attention that year. One irate lakeshore resident had gone so far as to appear before the county commissioners, saying he wanted to complain about the sheriff. But when he was told he'd have to state his complaint in an open meeting, he backed off.

Van Hoosier had investigated the rural crimes, of course, and he'd been the law officer who took the erring cashier into custody. He'd announced that he was going to run for office again, and his supporters had held a fund-raiser for him in July.

There was nothing that seemed to tie in with my mom's aborted wedding, her fiancé's death, and her flight from Warner Pier. Information about that was more likely to be found in the *Warner Pier Gazette.*

I looked at my watch. The library was going to close in a few minutes. I didn't have time to look at the fifty-two *Gazette*s that would have been published that year. But maybe I could look at Bill Dykstra's local obituary.

I rewound the *News* files, replaced them in their drawer, and found the *Gazette* files for August. Bill's suicide had rated a news story on page one. His obituary had run a week later, discreetly omitting the cause of death listed openly in the earlier story.

I learned nothing new about Bill's life. I already knew the names of his parents, and I had an outline of his educational career. What else is there to know about a twenty-year-old guy? The only surprise came in the list of bearers, the traditional six friends picked to escort the casket to the grave. These were still listed in Warner Pier obituaries in the early 1970s.

Three names I'd never heard before led the list. Either I didn't know them, or they had moved away from Warner Pier. I wrote them down. One of today's local businessmen came next — Thomas Hilton from the Garden Shop. Then there were two whose identities surprised me. Raleigh Taylor and Jason Foster.

Hmmm. Rollie, of course, would have worked with Bill's mother. So maybe he was a fairly logical choice as a bearer, though he would have been older than Bill.

But Jason Foster? How did he get in the lineup?

Jason is a fairly close friend of mine, a fellow foodie and a great guy. He had worked for years as a waiter, bartender, and restaurant manager for Mike Herrera, Warner Pier's mayor. He had recently severed ties with Mike and had submitted the winning bid to lease a restaurant on property owned by the Village of Warner Pier. This restaurant was located in the enormous house that Joe's ex-wife had built, on the property Joe had given to the city to be developed as a conference center.

The thing that made Jason a surprising choice as a bearer — thirty years ago — was that Jason is openly gay. Now, Warner Pier has a sizable gay community, but thirty years ago he might have been an outcast, unless he was keeping the closet door firmly shut.

I'd known Jason several years, and he'd never mentioned that he'd known my mother's fiancé. He was probably being tactful.

But how had Jason wound up as a bearer at Bill Dykstra's funeral? Were they family friends? Heck, they could be related. I didn't know the family tree for everybody in Warner Pier. Even nearly three years in the town, I was continually being surprised to learn that people I knew were related — sometimes after I'd made a comment about one of them to the other. It's never safe to talk about *anybody* in a small town.

But I could sure ask Jason about Bill Dykstra.

The librarian made her closing-time announcement, and I put the microfilm back in the cabinet and left. I put calling Jason at the top of my mental to do list for the next morning.

Then I drove by Joe's apartment to see if there was a light in the window. Nope. But on down the street I saw that there were cars at City Hall, so apparently the city council meeting hadn't adjourned yet. On an impulse, I parked my van at the curb and went inside.

Warner Pier's City Hall is in yet another of the town's classic Victorian structures, and the council chamber is up a steep flight of stairs. I tried to slip in quietly, but the swinging door to the chamber made a soft noise not unlike an elephant trumpeting in the distance, and every head in the room swung toward me. Joe grinned — he looked happy to see me, bless him — and our mayor, Mike Herrera, gave me a wave. I drew nods from Rollie, who was speaking, and most of the other seven council members as I sat down in a folding chair in the back row.

I tried to look intelligent while Rollie described a grant that was being awarded to Warner Pier, a grant that would mean the summer recreation program could continue at the current level. It had faced cutbacks, Rollie said, but the grant from the McKay Foundation would allow the continuation of nature walks and beach activities.

Mike Herrera heard Rollie's announcement with a complacent smile. He'd obviously known about it and was allowing Rollie to claim the credit.

"These grants from the McKay Foundation continue to amaze me," Mike said.

"Quinn McKay may not come to Warner Pier often anymore," Rollie said, "but he spent all his childhood summers here."

Mike shook his head. "That time we went to Chicago to meet with him — when we asked for a million for the conference center — he said he was unlikely to ever be back. So, Rollie, I want to know — just what do you have on the McKay Foundation? You used to cite them as one of the worst polluters on the Great Lakes."

"That was in the old days, when Benson McKay the Third was in charge," Rollie said. "Since Quinn took over, they've become good corporate citizens."

"Well, they never turn you down."

Rollie grinned. "I'm just lucky with money, you know, because of my initials."

"R.T.?"

"My middle initial is A, Mike. You know that if your initials spell a word, you'll get money. And my initials spell a word both ways."

Mike laughed. "Rat and tar," he said. "Some words. But you've done a lot for the city, Rollie, by getting this grant and the others you've obtained from the McKay Foundation, and we appreciate it."

Mike led a round of applause, then called for a vote on the consent agenda, the routine items. Unless there were some question about one of those, the council was on its final vote. This gave me only a moment to feel guilty about the way I'd snapped at Rollie Taylor the last time I'd seen him — a week earlier at the library. Did I owe him an apology? I couldn't decide.

There were no questions. Within three minutes Mike Herrera gave a sharp rap with his gavel and declared the meeting adjourned. I stayed where I was, waiting for Joe to finish any final bits of discussion with the council or the city clerk and still considering whether or not I'd been rude to Rollie.

Joe was still up front, talking to Mike Herrera, when Rollie came down the aisle. "Hi, Lee," he said. "Did you know that if Dolly Parton married Salvador Dalí, she'd be Dolly Dalí?"

"Sure," I said. "And if Aunt Nettie's chief assistant, Dolly Jolly, married Buddy Holly, she'd be Dolly Jolly Holly. But Rollie, I think I owe you an apology."

He raised his eyebrows. "What for?"

"For getting snappy at the library the other night. I don't have any real excuse for my rudeness."

"Forget it! Listen, do you and Joe like musical comedy?"

"I like it, and I've never heard him object to it. Why?"

"I'm sure you know that the touring company of *The Music Man* is coming to Grand Rapids. I've wound up with a couple of tickets I can't use. Let me give them to you."

"Give" them to us? I was amazed. Rollie never gave anything away. He'd had a garage sale when he got rid of his old clothes. It hadn't seemed to occur to him he could give them to the Salvation Army with almost no effort, and the garage sale meant he had to work all day to make twenty or twenty-five dollars.

After my initial surprise, I realized neither Joe nor I would be happy owing Rollie a favor. "We couldn't accept them, Rollie!" I said. "But it's awfully nice of you to offer."

"You'd be doing me a favor, Lee. I bought the tickets because the Holland Theater Guild was selling them as a fund-raiser. I thought I'd go, but it's the same night I agreed to work at the Kiwanis pancake supper."

"You can trade shifts with some other Kiwanian, Rollie. I know those tickets weren't cheap. You should use them yourself."

He and I argued back and forth for a few minutes. No, Rollie couldn't trade them back to the Holland Theater Guild; he was booked all five of the nights the show was going to play Grand Rapids. One night was city council, one was his Scout troop, one was the Kiwanis supper, the fourth was the Habitat for Humanity board meeting, and every Sunday afternoon he ran the bingo at a Dorinda senior citizen's residence. He swore he couldn't fail to appear for any of the activities.

We were still arguing when Joe came up. I explained what was going on.

Rollie smiled at Joe. "It ought to be a good show. And, honest, I can't use the tickets."

Joe offered to buy them, but Rollie again refused.

"You could scalp them," Joe said.

"How? The best place for that would be outside the theater, and I can't go that night."

"Okay, Rollie. Let's make a deal. We'll take the tickets, and in May I'll help you put your boat in the water."

"Done!" Rollie turned to me. "See, Lee. It's a win-win deal. You and Joe get the tickets, and I get professional help with my boat."

Rollie did have two extravagances — a

snazzy powerboat and European travel.

We were all happy. Rollie handed over the tickets, and we talked about what a great show *The Music Man* is and how Joe and I would have to eat lunch instead of dinner at the Kiwanis event — we assured Rollie that we didn't want to miss those yummy pancakes.

Everything was absolutely rosy until Chuck O'Riley came by. He'd been talking to the city clerk, apparently checking out something about the council meeting, and he came bouncing down the center aisle, beaming.

"Hey!" he said. "I found out about that old sheriff you were looking for, Lee. The old codger may still be alive."

CHAPTER 8

Chuck had blurted out the news of my search for information about the former sheriff at the top of his voice, right in the middle of the Warner Pier City Council chambers. All the city council members, the city clerk, the police chief, three retirees who had nothing to do but hang around City Hall — they'd all heard him. So had Joe, and I hadn't told Joe I was trying to find out what had happened to Sheriff Carl Van Hoosier.

I could have strangled Chuck. Instead, I nearly strangled myself, choking on my own tongue. "Oh! Chuck! Oh! Goshdarn! I didn't want you to go to a lot of trumpets over my idiotic curfew."

Chuck blinked, looking amazed, and I quickly tried to repair the damage. "I mean, I didn't want you to go to a lot of trouble over my idle curiosity!"

But before I could finish saying the last

word, Chuck was talking again, still at the top of his voice. "I really feel stupid about this, Lee. Finding him was the easiest thing in the world. Why I didn't think of it right away, I'll never know."

I was speechless by then, but Joe gave Chuck the cue he was angling for. "How did you find him, Chuck?"

"In the phone book! Can you believe it? Lee struggled through that microfilm for two hours, and she'd barely walked out when I thought of the phone book. And there he was, at Eighteen-hundred West Michigan Avenue, Dorinda. And that's an address everybody knows!"

I didn't know it, and my face must have shown my ignorance.

Chuck bounced with delight. "It's the retirement center!" he said. "The old guy must be in the nursing home. Pleasant Creek Senior Apartments and Nursing Center!"

"Oh," I said. "I know where that is, of course, on the west side of Dorinda. But I didn't know the street address."

Rollie entered the conversation at that point. "Are you talking about Carl Van Hoosier? The former sheriff?"

Chuck nodded, still grinning proudly.

"Carl is one of my regulars for bingo,"

Rollie said. "He had a stroke a year ago. He has trouble walking, uses a wheelchair. But he handles three bingo cards pretty easily."

Rollie turned to me then, and he asked the question I didn't want to answer. "Why are you looking for him, Lee?"

I didn't want to answer, but the whole situation was going to deteriorate even more if I didn't. "Oh, I was just looking up maternal — I mean, material! — material on the mystery — I mean, history! I was getting material on the history of Warner County."

"You didn't mention that." Chuck looked incredulous. As well he might, since I'd just created my interest in local history on the spot. "Are you doing a club program or something?"

A club program? He'd given me an out. I nearly snatched at the ready-made excuse, but I thought better of it. I was in enough trouble without lying any more.

"No, Chuck," I said. "Actually, the item about Van Hoosier in your twenty-five-years-ago column simply made me curious. I wondered what kind of crime a Warner County sheriff would have to be accused of before he was forced to perspire. I mean, retire!"

Chuck looked disappointed, and Rollie

gave a smile so happy his eyes all but disappeared. "Whatever Carl Van Hoosier did twenty-five years ago," he said, "he's just a harmless old coot now."

Joe earned my undying gratitude by taking my arm and turning me toward the door. "How about a pizza?" he said. "I never got any dinner."

"I grabbed a sandwich," I said, "but I could probably manage a couple of slices of pizza." We said good-bye to Rollie and Chuck, then walked out of the council chambers and down the stairs. We were both silent until we got in my van and I had started the motor.

"I assume you want to go to the Dock Street," I said, naming Warner Pier's pizza place.

"Sure," Joe said. "And on the way you can tell me what you were really doing looking at microfilm about Sheriff Carl Van Hoosier."

I sighed as I put the van in gear and pulled out from the curb. "I told Rollie the absolute truth," I said. "I saw the item in the newspaper, and I got curious. You understand why I got curious, I'm sure, since you know what my mom said. So I went over to the *Gazette* to look up the original article. It didn't tell me much, so I went to the library

107

to look at more microfilm."

"What did you find out?"

"Not a darn thing about Van Hoosier! The good ol' boys of twenty-five years ago were just as adept at cover-ups as the good ol' boys of today are. The commissioners must have had the goods on Van Hoosier, because he did resign, but nothing was made public."

"Who was on the commission in those days?"

"I'd have to look at the few notes I made. I didn't recognize any of the names."

Joe was silent, apparently thinking, until I parked in front of the Dock Street Pizza Place, Warner Pier's social center. As soon as I turned off the motor, he turned to me. "Listen, Lee," he said, "if you really want to know what the in-crowd thought about Van Hoosier, you need to talk to one of the good ol' boys from twenty-five years ago."

"I can see that, Joe. But are any of them still alive?"

"Sure. I can think of one right now."

"Who?"

"Mac McKay. He was county attorney for years. You remember, I did an internship with him." Joe opened his door and swung his feet out. "We're still friends. In fact, I should have taken you over to meet him before this. I'll give him a call."

That remark called for action, and I took it. I grabbed a fistful of the sleeve of Joe's down jacket and pulled him toward me. "Just come back in this van and close that door," I said.

He obeyed, looking slightly puzzled. "Just what did I say?"

"Exactly the right thing, you big lunk." I planted my best kiss on him, right on the mouth.

About three minutes later, Joe spoke. "Maybe I don't need a pizza, after all."

I sat back. "Oh, yes, you do. I want you in top form, at full strength. You can't do your best work on an empty stomach."

"Are you going to tell me what inspired this desire for my 'best work' right at this moment?"

"Because you reminded me of one of the reasons I love you. You're just as nosy as I am! You want to know why my mom ran away from Warner Pier, too."

Joe laughed. "You can't blame me for wanting to know if the runaway-bride gene is implanted in your DNA."

"It's not. You're not getting rid of me, no matter what. But we can plan the rest of the night later. Right now let's go in and order a pizza, and I'll tell you what I found out at the library."

"I thought you didn't find out anything."

"I didn't find out anything about Sheriff Van Hoosier. I found out a few other things."

Twenty minutes later we were eating a pepperoni pizza with mushrooms and drinking Labatt Blue. Luckily, the Dock Street Pizza Place is quiet, at least in the winter, and I'd been able to talk without yelling as I told Joe the scraps of information I'd found out, including the names of the bearers at Bill Dykstra's funeral. He'd agreed that we had several new leads for information.

"I'm uneasy about approaching Rollie," I said. "I just don't know him that well."

"I can talk to Rollie," Joe said. "And I'll call Mac McKay. Mac's been around Warner County forever. Knows where all the bodies are buried."

"McKay?" I thought a minute. "He's not related to the McKay clan over here, is he?"

"Maybe a second or third cousin. I think that the rich McKay family did come from Warner County originally. Seems as if that cottage they have is on the family's original farm. Mac would be a poor relation. He's just a small-town attorney who's got no more ambition than I have. Does it matter?"

"Probably not. Some of the McKays buy chocolate from us."

Joe went on. "If we go over to Dorinda to see Mac, we can stop at the nursing home and take a look at Carl Van Hoosier."

"But, Joe . . ."

"What?"

"I don't really want to talk to Van Hoosier. What could I ask him? 'Did you run my mother out of town?' That sounds pretty silly."

"We could ask him if he remembers the Dykstra suicide."

"I guess so." I wasn't convinced. "I guess it won't hurt to stop at the nursing home. Inez Deacon has an apartment there, and I haven't been over in ages. And I'll call Jason first thing tomorrow — or as soon as he's likely to be up — and ask him how he happened to know Bill Dykstra."

We had divided the jobs. I was to talk to Jason. Joe was to talk to Rollie and set up an appointment with Mac McKay. On our way back from Dorinda, we'd stop at the nursing home. It was all arranged before we went back to Joe's apartment and resumed the scene that had begun in the van.

But the plan got all "back-ass-wards," as my dad would say.

First, when I called Jason's home around

ten a.m. the next day, I got the answering machine. When I called his restaurant, I got a waiter who told me Jason was in Chicago buying equipment and wouldn't be back until the next day.

And Joe didn't have a lot more luck than I did. Rollie didn't answer his phone. Mac McKay said he was glad to hear from Joe, but he had Rotary Club at noon, followed by the library board.

"So he invited us over for dinner," Joe said. "His house at five o'clock. If we leave about three, we should have time to stop at the retirement center, see Inez for a while, and peek in at Carl Van Hoosier."

"But we won't have talked to Mac yet."

Joe and I discussed whether or not it was important for us to quiz Mac McKay about Van Hoosier before we tackled the former sheriff.

"Listen," I said finally. "It may be that Carl Van Hoosier isn't fit to be interviewed. But if I get over toward Dorinda, I need to stop and see Inez, whether I talk to anybody else at Pleasant Creek or not."

We left it at that. Aunt Nettie made up a gift box of Inez's favorite chocolates, Dutch caramel bonbons ("creamy European-style caramel in a dark chocolate shell") and maple cream truffles ("a milk chocolate

112

truffle flavored with sweet maple"). Joe came by at three o'clock, and we headed out on the two-lane blacktop road that connects Warner Pier to the east side of Warner County.

It was a beautiful, crisp day — cold, but sunny. The roads were clear, if you don't count that slushy mess along the edges, and Joe and I were in high spirits. I think we both felt that we were doing something a bit naughty; we were sticking our noses into a situation that wasn't really any of our business.

Pleasant Creek Senior Apartments is in a red brick building with white Georgian pillars. Residents furnish their own apartments — most of them one-room, with an entrance through a hall that has a galley kitchen on one side and the bathroom door on the other. Meals are served in a central dining room, and there are lots of activities — exercise classes, trips, and movies every evening. Inez Deacon seemed to be contented, and I figured that if the notoriously independent Inez could make a home there, the place must be genuinely nice.

Inez Deacon had taught at a Holland high school until her retirement more than twenty years earlier. She'd lived a block or so down Lake Shore Drive from Aunt Nettie for twenty-five or more years. She loved the lake, and every day she'd walk up and down the beach, picking up trash as she checked out the birds, the wind direction, the height of the waves, the rounded stones along the edge of the water. But Inez had had her first heart problems more than fifteen years earlier, and now her "bum pump," as she always called it, had caught up with her. She was having heart failure. She was growing weaker all the time, and she'd decided it was best to move to a spot where she could get assistance readily.

But her personality was as lively as ever. She was sitting beside her window when Joe and I knocked at the open door of her apartment, then walked through the narrow hallway. She turned to look at us with her finger to her lips. "Shh! There's a robin outside here. Tiptoe over and don't make any sudden moves."

We obeyed silently and were rewarded with a look at a bright-eyed, red-breasted bird not three feet outside Inez's window. It lingered nearly a full minute, scratching in the snow, then flew away.

Inez gave a sort of gasp, and I realized we'd all been holding our breaths. She turned to us then. "Lee! Joe! I'm so glad you saw my robin! So few of them stay in

Michigan all winter. It's always nice to have a witness."

She embraced us both, then waved us to chairs. "I thought I wouldn't see you two until the wedding."

"We're counting on you to be there, Inez," I said. "After all, if it weren't for you, I'd still be sitting around pouting, and Joe wouldn't even have wanted to marry me."

She gave a snort. "You'd have quit pouting on your own," she said. "I was just incidental." But I could tell she was pleased by my comment.

Inez and I had become friends during the summer I was sixteen. My parents were getting a divorce, my mom was moving from Prairie Creek to Dallas, and I was to transfer from a high school of 250 students to one with 2,500. My mother was busy job hunting, and my dad, I realize today, was becoming involved with Annie, who's now his wife. In desperation, my mom packed me off to Warner Pier to spend the summer working for her brother and sister-in-law in their chocolate shop.

I was not happy to be there. I was not happy with my parents. I was not happy with one single thing in my life. Then I met Inez walking on the beach. Maybe she understood teenagers because of her years of teaching. Or maybe she and I simply hit it off. Anyway, she did a lot of listening and a little advising, and by the end of the summer I had the confidence to tackle a Dallas high school, to cope with my problem parents, and to accept the unconditional love Aunt Nettie and Uncle Phil were offering me. I'd also been involved in a crime, helping to identify a kidnapper and hit-and-run driver who'd nearly killed Inez.

It was hard to see Inez losing her energy. But that day she looked pretty good, and I told her so.

"I feel fine most of the time," she said. "It's just getting harder to breathe. I use oxygen sometimes. But I'm going to dance at your wedding."

"I'm counting on you for a polka," Joe said.

We told her about the wedding plans, and she laughed at my account of Aunt Nettie's redecorating ideas. I answered questions about her old neighbors. She opened the chocolates from Aunt Nettie and offered us a piece. We both declined.

"You have one," I said. "If it won't ruin your dinner."

Inez smiled. "I think I will have one whether it ruins my dinner or not. The bum pump is denying me enough of life's plea-

116

sures. Now tell me about Timothy Hart. Has he managed to stay on the wagon?"

"Well, he hasn't come staggering down Lake Shore Drive lately," I said. But Inez's questions about the neighbors had made me think of her in a different light. "Inez, did you know my mother?"

"I met her when she came for Phil's funeral, Lee. But she had left home before I moved to Lake Shore Drive."

"Oh."

I must have sounded dispirited, because Inez frowned. "You're not fighting with her again, are you?"

It was Joe who spoke. "Lee had never known that her mother ran off on her wedding day, Inez. She just found out, and she'd like to understand why."

"Have you asked her?"

"It's hard on the telephone," I said. "Especially since she never mentioned the episode to me. But she's coming for the wedding, so maybe we can talk then. She did ask one question that puzzled me. She wanted to know about the former sheriff, Carl Van Hoosier."

Inez frowned. "His apartment is in this wing, but I don't talk with him much."

"He's not in the nursing wing?"

"No. He had a stroke and uses a wheelchair, but he still has his apartment. And it's nice — one of the doubles. And don't let that dumb act he does sometimes fool you!"

"What do you mean?"

"Oh, I've seen him pull it. If he doesn't want to talk about something — who made the mess in the puzzle room, maybe — he acts as if he's out of it. But when the staff aide is gone, he gets this sly look." Inez nodded vigorously. "You know, my grandmother always said that cranky old people were cranky young people. And I'd guess that *crafty* old people were *crafty* young people. Van Hoosier always had that reputation, and from what I've seen of him, he's as sneaky as he ever was."

After a few more minutes Joe and I said good-bye. Inez didn't offer to walk us out. She had grown noticeably more short of breath as we talked.

Joe took my hand as we walked down the hall. "It's sad to see Inez growing feeble," he said. "She's such a stout character it's hard to realize she won't last forever."

I nodded and blinked back a few tears. "She's still interested in everything around her, though. Did you notice that she claimed she didn't talk with Carl Van Hoosier, but she knew just how he treated the staff?"

"She hasn't lost her powers of observation. And how about *your* powers of observation? Do you want to take a peek at Van Hoosier?"

"Well, since we're here . . ."

Joe stopped at the reception desk and asked for Van Hoosier's apartment number. Then we went back down Inez's wing. Van Hoosier's apartment was at the end.

"Twenty-two east," Joe said. "This is it."

"Should we go in?"

"Sure," Joe murmured quietly. "Like I said, we can always ask him if he remembers the Bill Dykstra suicide."

Joe tapped on the door. Like most of the doors in the retirement center, it was standing open. But there was no response to Joe's knock.

Joe raised his eyebrows and tapped again. "Sheriff Van Hoosier? May we come in?"

He took two steps into the apartment, steps that took him into the little hallway with the galley kitchen along one side and the bathroom door on the other. I followed him closely. Somehow I didn't want to get too far away from him in the alien environment of Carl Van Hoosier's apartment.

Joe gasped. He took three giant steps into the apartment itself, then dropped to his knees.

The first thing I saw was an overturned wheelchair behind Joe. It took me a moment to realize Joe was kneeling beside a large man who was stretched out on the floor beside that wheelchair.

"Call the nurse!" Joe said.

I scanned the room and found a white cord attached to an emergency switch. I yanked it.

"Should we try CPR?"

Joe looked up at me. His hand was on the man's neck, apparently feeling for a pulse. "I think he's already dead."

Chocolate Chat:
Childhood Chocolate — Part I

As a child during World War II, I was aware of only a few of the sacrifices that civilians were making for the effort to win the war.

The main one, as far as I was concerned, was chocolate.

All the chocolate, we were told, was going to soldiers and sailors overseas. Chocolate bars were in short supply for children.

Across the street from Franklin Elementary School in Ardmore, Oklahoma, was a small mom-and-pop grocery where all us kids would blow our spending money. On the rare occasion when the store got a few boxes of Hershey's bars, they would all be sold before the first bell rang for the school day.

I was a last-minute scholar, dashing into class just as the bell rang. Even if I had a nickel, I was never early enough to get a Hershey's bar.

Both my parents liked chocolate. I remember the glee with which my father, after the war, introduced me to the Valomilk Cup, still my favorite form of marshmallow cream, and the Cherry Mash. Then we knew the war was really over.

— *JoAnna Carl*

CHAPTER 9

"I'll find some help!"

I ran out of the apartment and down the hall toward the reception desk, the nearest place where I knew I could find a staff member. As I got there a completely bald man in a white uniform was walking rapidly toward me, coming through the lounge behind the desk; I knew the nursing-home wing was back that way.

I guessed that the bald man was answering the emergency line in Van Hoosier's room. I ran to meet him.

"It's Carl Van Hoosier!" I said. "He's not breathing!"

The man's rapid walk became a run, and he barreled past me without a word. I followed him at a fast walk. When I got back to Van Hoosier's apartment, he and Joe were both kneeling beside the old sheriff, and the bald man had his stethoscope in place.

"I didn't try CPR," Joe said.

The bald man took the stethoscope out of his ears. "He has a do-not-resuscitate order in place," he said.

I stood by the door, feeling shaky. After all my curiosity about Van Hoosier, I certainly hadn't expected to find him dead. Of course, I wasn't grieved by his death; I'd never met the man, and what I'd heard about him didn't make me sorry that we weren't acquainted. But it seemed extremely odd.

That's when I began to look around the apartment. And the situation began to seem even odder.

I'd already seen that Van Hoosier's wheelchair was on its side. A small table was turned over, too. A floor lamp had been smashed. A throw rug was crumpled up. A metal candy dish was in the middle of the floor, and Hershey's Kisses were all over the place. A lightweight side chair had also been knocked over, and that chair was clear across the room from the wheelchair.

"Listen, y'all," I said. "This room doesn't look like some old guy died peacefully. It looks like a fight went on first!"

Joe stood up and looked around. "I suppose it's possible that he thrashed around in his final moments. But I don't see how he could have done this much damage."

The bald guy stood up. Now I could see his name tag: PRIDDY, RN. He looked around the room. "It does look odd," he said.

He knelt again. This time he pulled Van Hoosier's lower eyelid down and looked at it closely. Joe dropped to his knees, too, and watched closely. The nurse felt Van Hoosier's throat, then looked at his head, feeling around it.

He looked at Joe, and Joe looked at him. They both seemed to be assimilating the situation.

Then Joe spoke. "I used to be a defense attorney. I represented a guy in a strangling case."

The nurse nodded and stood up.

"This is too weird," he said. His voice was quiet; I had the sense he was speaking to himself. "He's got a contusion on his temple, too. Who would want to bash the old bastard, then smother him?"

Priddy, RN, seemed to come to himself. "Sorry," he said. "That wasn't a very professional comment. I'll call his doctor."

"Lee and I had better wait down the hall, in case this turns out to be a crime scene," Joe said. "We won't leave until we find out if anybody wants our names."

The bald man raised a hand. "Please," he

said, "don't say anything!"

Joe nodded.

When we got back to the reception area, a middle-aged guy in a suit came rushing out of an office marked "Administrator" and nearly knocked us both flat, so I gathered that Nurse Priddy had called his boss to say they'd had a death. A suspicious death.

The receptionist, who was not concealing her interest in the proceedings very well, told us that we could get coffee in the main lounge, in an area behind her. We said we'd wait there. Joe used his cell phone to call Mac McKay and tell him we might be late for dinner. Then we found seats where we could see the comings and goings.

And there were lots of comings and goings. A man Joe recognized as a Dorinda doctor came rushing in the main door within ten minutes. Not long after that Priddy and the administrator put their heads together near the receptionist's desk and talked in low voices. We couldn't hear them, but there was a lot of vigorous gesturing and scowling. The administrator ended it by shaking his head and going to stare out the entrance, arms folded, anger in his shoulders and neck. Apparently the doctor had agreed with Priddy about the suspicious nature of Van Hoosier's death, because a sheriff's car pulled up out front, and almost immediately after that a Michigan State Police car drove up. The administrator met them, glaring and talking vigorously. He didn't seem to approve of murder in one of his nice apartments.

There were no sirens, but the residents of Pleasant Creek knew something was up. A crowd was gathering in the lounge — two old ladies leaning on walkers, a man bent almost in two by osteoporosis, a couple who sat down at a card table and pretended to play gin rummy, assorted women who gathered in clusters and eyed the activities. A few of the people obviously lived in Van Hoosier's wing, and they made periodic forays down the hall to see what was going on, then came back to report.

I guess we were gawking as much as the Pleasant Creek residents, because I nearly jumped out of my skin when someone behind me called my name.

"Lee? Joe? What are you two doing here?"

I turned to see Rollie Taylor, grinning from ear to ear as usual.

"Rollie?" I said. "I didn't expect to see you."

"It's bingo day," Rollie said. "And, Lee, did you know that if Bea Arthur married Sting, she'd be Bea Sting?"

I rolled my eyes and groaned. "I thought you said you called bingo on Sundays."

"And on alternate Wednesdays." Rollie gestured at the assembled crowd of residents. "These folks usually go straight from bingo to dinner. What's going on?"

I let Joe tell him. I didn't want to think about the scene in Van Hoosier's apartment. I walked over to the window and looked out at the wintry scene. I was beginning to dread the next act in this little drama. Anytime now a representative of either the Warner County Sheriff's Office or the Michigan State Police was going to find out who had discovered Carl Van Hoosier's body. And they were going to want to know why two complete strangers had dropped by to see the old guy.

And I didn't have the slightest idea how to answer that question. It wasn't that I wanted to lie. It was just that the reason we'd come was going to sound so stupid.

I stood there, staring at the snow and stewing until my nerves had turned into needles and were poking holes in my skin. I barely acknowledged Rollie's good-bye, and when Joe joined me by the window, I clutched at his sleeve as if I were grabbing a lifeline.

"Joe, is there any kind of a sensible lie we

can come up with?"

"What do we need to lie about?"

"About why we went into Carl Van Hoosier's apartment. Neither of us ever met the guy before."

Joe grinned. "I'll play the city attorney card. Maybe it will work."

"You can't claim you were on any kind of official business!"

"I know. But they'll be polite." He gave me a one-armed hug. "Relax."

A few more minutes went by, and the bald nurse came through the lounge. When he saw us, he came over. Joe stuck out his hand in shaking position.

"I'm Joe Woodyard," he said. "This is my fiancée, Lee McKinney. We didn't exactly get a chance to introduce ourselves in there."

The tall nurse shook hands with both of us. "Elmer Priddy," he said. "Thanks for waiting around."

Priddy looked troubled, as well he might, I guess. He was around an inch taller than Joe, but thin, and had a square jaw. I guessed his age at midfifties. His head had been shaved, rather than being naturally bald, and I could see the five o'clock shadow that marked the boundaries of where his hairline would have been. Most guys who shave their heads are almost bald anyway, I've noticed. They apparently just decide to give up the fight. But Priddy's hair grew down low onto his forehead and when he ducked his head I saw that the five o'clock shadow looked even all over his skull.

"I'm a lawyer," Joe said. "I've been involved with a couple of murder trials. I'm far from expert, but I didn't like the way that apartment looked."

Priddy shook his head. "If it weren't for the eyelids, I might have said natural causes. And then I found that bump."

Joe went on. "I guess the doctor agreed with you."

"The administrator doesn't like it, but there's going to be an autopsy."

"That's smart," Joe said. "Even if it shows natural causes . . ." We all nodded wisely.

"Any idea when he died?" Joe sounded idly curious.

"According to the body temp . . . I'd be guessing. But CPR wouldn't have helped him." Priddy looked at us closely. "You weren't relatives of Van Hoosier's?"

"No. We didn't know him at all," Joe said. "I'm city attorney over at Warner Pier. We were looking for a little information about an old case."

Priddy's head snapped toward Joe, and

his eyes grew wide. But it was a moment before he spoke. "He probably wouldn't have remembered," he said. "I guess I'd better get back to work."

He walked back the way I'd seen him come, down the hall that led to the nursing wing.

A few more minutes later one of the sheriff's deputies came out. He checked with the receptionist first, consulting the check-in sheet we'd signed as we arrived. I felt relieved as I realized we had some sort of proof of when we got there.

Then he came over to talk to us. Joe's prediction turned out to be fairly accurate. The deputy merely asked for our names and addresses. We each gave him a business card and told him we weren't relatives of Van Hoosier's. He seemed to assume that we'd dropped by on a social visit.

Joe fished for more details. He explained that he'd spent some time as a defense attorney and without saying too much made it clear that he'd recognized the symptoms of violent death in Carl Van Hoosier's apartment.

"The furniture turned over," he said, "and the eyelids."

The deputy nodded. "Yeah, the doctor . . ." Then he apparently decided he was saying too much to witnesses, and he broke off. "But we won't know anything until there's an autopsy. You guys can go. We know where to find you."

I hardly had to say a word, but I still managed to goof it up. "Good lie," I said. "I mean, good-bye!"

The deputy blinked, but he let us go.

By then it was past six p.m., and the Michigan winter night had arrived. It was with great relief that I walked across Pleasant Creek's brightly lit parking lot and climbed into Joe's truck.

"I hope your friend Mac McKay isn't a teetotaler," I said. "I could sure use a drink."

Joe laughed and put the truck into reverse. He backed up, then suddenly hit the brakes. A horn blasted.

A ramshackle pickup truck, its bed loaded with plastic garbage bags, was behind us. The driver was shaking her fist at us and her lips were moving. I assumed she was cursing.

In the bright lights of the lot, the driver was easy to see. She wore a white knit cap with a bright red pom-pom. It was Lovie Dykstra.

Joe and I watched as she drove away. "I guess Lovie's got the concession for Pleasant Creek's aluminum cans," Joe said. He turned out of the parking lot and went on toward Dorinda.

Dorinda is a pleasant little town filled with Victorian houses. We went through a nice little business district which clustered around the courthouse. There was a bank, a small supermarket, a hardware store, a mom-and-pop restaurant, a drugstore, an everything-a-dollar store. Signs indicated that Warner County's lawyers had offices above the bank and in one renovated professional building. Then we crossed the railroad tracks and passed a fruit warehouse, a cannery — shut down for the winter — and a farmer's co-op building. There was almost no traffic at six thirty on a Wednesday evening.

Superficially Dorinda had some resemblance to Warner Pier. Most of its buildings dated from the same era, for example. But the cultural divide was wide. Dorinda was definitely a farming community. In comparison, Warner Pier was Sophisticated City. While Warner Pier was not any more lively than Dorinda in the winter, our business district was larger and was lined with art galleries, bookshops, gift stores, snazzy clothing boutiques, winery outlets, and a shop that made and sold fancy chocolates, businesses of a type Dorinda lacked completely. True, Warner Pier had a hardware store, but it featured more barbecue grills than plywood, just as our marine salesrooms offered more cabin cruisers than fiberglass fishing boats.

Joe and I had driven only thirty miles, but we'd crossed a tribal boundary.

Mac McKay lived in a pleasant house that sat on a little knoll in a nice neighborhood. The house was painted light gray, with neat black shutters, and Mac McKay himself was waiting at the door.

I loved him on sight. He was a small man — he came about to my shoulder — with a few wisps of white hair. His eyes twinkled and his smile beamed, and he greeted Joe with obvious pleasure. He took my hand with real warmth.

"Welcome, Lee! You look as if you're as wonderful as Joe claims you are."

"You look wonderful, too, Mr. McKay. Could I give you a hug?"

"Only if you'll call me 'Mac' afterward."

"Of course! Anybody I'm on hugging terms with gets called by their first name."

The hug turned out to be a joint effort, and Mac stood on tiptoe to give me a kiss on the cheek. He called out to someone in the kitchen, then hung up our coats and led us into a living room where a cheery fire burned. I seemed to raise myself further in his esteem by oohing and ahing over the handmade tiles that surrounded the fireplace. Each showed a different Michigan wildflower.

"My late wife made those," Mac said. "She was quite an artist."

A Hispanic housekeeper brought in a tray of canapés and a bottle of wine. Mac fussed about, pouring wine for me and scotch for Joe. Joe hates scotch, but he took it with a small grin. To a lawyer of Mac McKay's age, scotch was the only suitable drink to offer a fellow attorney.

Mac made sure I was seated close to the fire; then he sat in a wing chair facing us, raising his own glass of scotch in a wordless toast. He leaned forward.

"What's this about you two finding that old reprobate Carl Van Hoosier dead?"

I gasped, but Joe only laughed. "So you've got a mole at Pleasant Creek."

"My former secretary lives there now. Ellen Thoms."

"I didn't see her. Why didn't she speak to me?"

"Vanity, my boy. Vanity. She's rather gnarled by arthritis these days, and she doesn't like to be caught using her walker. But what happened to Carl? Ellen said our current sheriff was there. In person."

Joe quickly sketched the scene we'd found when we dropped in on Van Hoosier. When he described how Nurse Priddy had examined the dead man, Mac raised his eyebrows.

"I'm surprised he didn't simply declare it a natural death," he said.

"I was surprised, too," Joe said. "I think the administrator recommended that finding, but Priddy stuck to his guns."

"Priddy said something about his throat," I said. "And he looked at his eyelids."

Mac nodded like the former prosecutor he was. "Strangulation or suffocation — the first one almost always crushes the windpipe. And either cause of death leaves tiny little broken blood vessels in the eyelids."

"Yeah," Joe said. "I thought I spotted the red specks."

"Maybe the nurse didn't think he could cover it up after you'd seen them."

"I think he'd made his mind up before he knew I'd seen the specks," Joe said. "Anyway, they're going to do an autopsy."

"It's poetic justice," Mac said.

Before we could ask him to explain, the housekeeper came in and said dinner was ready.

"We'll analyze Carl later," Mac said. He

led us into the dining room for a delicious dinner of beef stew, salad, and crusty rolls. While we ate, Mac made sure we kept the conversation general. He obviously was interested in a wide range of subjects, and he'd kept in touch with his former profession, displaying an up-to-the-minute knowledge about changes in the Michigan law on zoning, for example. The food was upper-Midwest home cooking, with a luscious *tres leches* cake for dessert as the only nod to the housekeeper's ethnicity. She left before we finished, so Joe and I cleared the table, but Mac insisted on loading the dishwasher himself. We took our coffee to the living room, and Mac put another log on the fire.

He sat in his easy chair looking expectant. "So, just what did you want to know about Carl Van Hoosier?"

Joe answered. "Why did he get bounced out of office?"

"Did one too many favors for my rich relatives."

Joe raised his eyebrows. "Then you *are* related to the McKay family who has the big place over at Warner Pier?"

"I'm a poor relation. My grandfather was a brother to Benson McKay, the great-grandfather of the current head of McKay Chemicals, Quinn McKay."

Joe looked confused, and I spoke up. "So you and the guy who's always giving Warner Pier grants are second cousins once removed."

"You know your genealogy, young lady. Not that the relationship matters to me. We've never had Thanksgiving dinner together or chatted at a family funeral. The connection is extremely remote. And after my round with Carl Van Hoosier, I assure you that the rich McKays want to keep it that way." Mac rubbed his hands together gleefully.

"When you were county attorney," Joe said, "you usually tried to get along with citizens, even citizens who were just summer people. Why do you feel differently about the McKays?"

"They got too blatant, Joe. They had bought old Carl, and maybe that wasn't a big deal when it came to a few speeding tickets or some extra security when they had a party. They'd been paying Van Hoosier off for little favors like that for years. But when it came to vehicular homicide, I drew the line."

"Who killed whom?"

"It was the father of Quinn, Benson the third. He was driving his Porsche, drunk, with a girl from another of the summer families along. Ben always liked young women, as the age of his widow testifies. She's just a year older than Quinn. Anyway, Ben hit a tree on Lake Shore Drive. Ben survived. The girl didn't."

"Rough on the girl and her family."

"Rough on the girl. I didn't have much sympathy for her family. Within a week of the funeral, they were giving signals that a major cash settlement would ease their grief substantially. But I thought Ben should stand trial. When I heard that Carl had lost the blood sample we needed to convict, I guess I lost my temper. From then on it was war between Carl Van Hoosier and me."

"How did you manage to win the war and get him out of office?"

"I got the state police behind me, subpoenaed Carl's bank records. Looked at property transfers. The McKays had sold Carl some property way below market value, and he resold it immediately. Made a killing." Mac shrugged. "I might never have convinced a jury, but I was able to put enough pressure on Carl to get him to resign. Besides, the public had had enough by the . And ol' Carl had made a big enough pile to retire on, so he went fairly quietly."

I leaned forward. "How about the rumor

that he would — well, exploit courting couples?"

"Handcuff the boy and rape the girl?" Mac frowned. "I know every kid in Warner County believed that, but I could never pin it down. I finally concluded it was a sort of Warner County folk tale. Especially when the rumor continued after Carl left office. And after his successor left office."

Joe nodded. "I admit I heard it when I was in high school, but I hadn't realized until recently that it was a continuation of the tale my mother had believed. So Van Hoosier's main problem was doing too many favors for the summer residents?"

"And accepting money for it — though we never proved exactly where the money came from. But pandering to the summer people is a stupid thing for a county official to do. The summer people don't vote here."

"Yeah," Joe said. "And the locals resent special treatment for them."

"Right. I wasn't able to send my second cousin to prison, but he managed to stay out of trouble until he died a couple of years later."

"Was this the father of the McKay who was kidnapped?"

Mac scowled. "Quinn," he said. "I've

always wondered if Benson was sorry he turned up alive."

CHAPTER 10

I guess my surprise showed, because Mac McKay looked a little embarrassed.

"I'm just repeating the gossip of the time," he said. "Talk along the lakeshore was that Ben the Third didn't approve of his son. But he seemed like a nice kid to me, thirty-four years ago."

"You knew him?" I'm sure I sounded surprised.

"He did an internship for me the summer before he was kidnapped." Then Mac smiled. "But we've gotten away from Carl Van Hoosier. Why do Carl's problems of twenty-five years ago have any interest for you two?"

Joe and I exchanged a glance. He shrugged slightly, tossing the ball to me. Telling Mac McKay the whole story was my option. Did I want to?

Mac seemed very trustworthy. I leaned forward and spoke. "I don't suppose you remember the suicide of a young man named Bill Dykstra?" I said. I told him the date.

Mac leaned back and scratched his head. "Was that the runaway-bride case?"

"Yes," I said. "I just recently found out that my mom *was* the runaway bride. She's never talked to me about it."

"And you'd like to know just what happened."

"Of course."

Mac sighed. "So would I. I always thought that whole situation was screwy, but I had no evidence, so I didn't feel that I could get involved. Bill Dykstra's parents were furious, of course, and I understood their attitude, since Bill Dykstra had no known history of drug abuse."

Drug abuse? I sat there rigid. I must have looked like a piece of Lake Michigan driftwood half-buried in sand. How did drug abuse figure in Bill Dykstra's death? Finally I gasped. Then I spoke. Or rather yelled.

"Drug abuse!"

Joe echoed my words, but he didn't yell. "Drug abuse? Mac, are you saying that Bill Dykstra had taken drugs?"

Mac nodded. "That's what the sheriff's report said. 'Drug paraphernalia' was found in the car with him."

"What kind of drugs?" Joe said.

"Oh, pot, as I recall. A roach and a small baggie, maybe. I'd have to look it up."

"That's a surprise," Joe said. "But I guess it shouldn't be."

Mac nodded. "Yes, thirty-odd years ago smoking pot was pretty common. But his parents hadn't known anything about it, and their older son had been picked up for possession, so I'd have expected them to recognize the symptoms. I think their reaction is the reason I remember the case — they were really shocked."

I got my voice back. "But Bill committed suicide by running a hose from his exhaust into his car. There was nothing in the newspaper report about drugs."

"He hadn't overdosed or anything, Lee. He'd simply smoked some pot. It makes some people depressed, you know. So he drove out to a lonely place, and — like you said — used a garden hose and some duct tape — both of them identified as coming from his parents' garage — to kill himself."

Joe frowned. "But where did Lee's mom fit in? Why did she run away?"

"Since nobody ever got to ask her, I have no idea. Maybe she realized he was taking drugs, decided she didn't want to be married to a druggie, and got on a bus." Mac turned to me. "Since Bill was dead by his own hand, and the drugs didn't appear to be directly connected to his death, maybe they weren't mentioned to the newspaper. Or the editor chose not to print it."

We left it at that. Joe and Mac caught up on a few people who had worked in the courthouse back when Joe had been an intern, then Joe and I excused ourselves and left. Mac assured us that he'd see us at our wedding reception. I was sure the feisty little guy would be the life of the party.

Neither Joe nor I had much to say as we drove back to Warner Pier. I was assimilating the things Mac had told us, especially the part about Bill Dykstra smoking pot. It just didn't seem possible. My mom had always been firmly against drugs of any sort. She had to be really sick before she took an aspirin. Maybe seeing her fiancé getting into the drug scene had made her run away. But, no, that wouldn't work because it didn't explain why she was terrified of Sheriff Carl Van Hoosier. The late Sheriff Carl Van Hoosier. Who, according to Mac McKay, had been run out of office because he did too many favors for Mac's "rich relatives."

The whole thing made my head spin.

Joe didn't ask me to come home with him; I guess he could tell I wasn't in a romantic mood. But after he pulled into Aunt Nettie's drive, he put both arms around me.

"You know what you've got to do, don't you?" he said.

I leaned against him and sighed. "Yeah. I've got to ask my mom what happened."

"Or drop the whole thing."

I laughed. "And leave my curiosity unsatisfied?"

"Life's always full of unanswered questions."

"Unless . . ." I hesitated, then spoke again. "I don't suppose that Carl Van Hoosier's death had anything to do with my asking questions."

Joe didn't answer for a moment. "I don't see how asking questions about something that happened more than thirty years ago could be a motive for killing the old guy today. From the sound of him, Van Hoosier would have gone on making enemies after he was out of office."

I kissed Joe good night and went inside. Aunt Nettie was in bed, but awake, so I went in to report on our evening. She was properly horrified by our discovery of Carl Van Hoosier's body, and listened sympathetically to my tale. But what she really wanted to know was how Inez was doing, and I was glad I could tell her Inez seemed

146

to be fine. She smiled as I described Mac McKay, with his lively interest in the happenings of "his" county — past and present.

"He more or less claimed to have forced Carl Van Hoosier out of office — all on his own," I said. "Said Van Hoosier did 'too many favors for my rich relatives.' McKay is a second cousin once removed to the heir to the McKay fortune, Quinn McKay."

"The one who was kidnapped?"

"Yep. Mac said he knew him, though he apparently doesn't associate with the family."

I told her what Mac had said about his relatives, and she nodded wisely. "I think the father — that would be Benson McKay the Third — was married several times," she said. "But the same Mrs. Benson McKay the Third has come into the shop ever since we opened, so I guess she's the widow. I think she inherited the summer cottage — or got a life interest in it or something."

"That may be the reason Quinn McKay doesn't come around here much. I was at city council last night, and the McKay Foundation had made a grant to the city. Apparently they've made a bunch of grants. If Quinn McKay doesn't even come up here, I wonder why they're interested in

Warner Pier projects."

"Maybe the stepmother is a foundation trustee."

"Maybe so. Is the McKay place that big modern thing on the river?"

"No, that's a different McKay family. They're from Detroit. The McKay cottage is about two miles south of this house and on the inland side of Lake Shore Drive. A big old farmhouse."

"The inland side? What? The McKays have all that money, and they haven't bought a view of the lake?"

Aunt Nettie smiled gently. "My understanding is that the house was inherited from the original McKay pioneers. It was the family farmhouse."

"Seems as if they would have traded up."

"Mrs. McKay could have inherited the cottage but not enough money to make major changes to it. She and her guests must swim at Badger Creek Beach. It's just across Lake Shore Drive."

Aunt Nettie yawned then, so I said good night. I went up to my room, sat on the edge of the bed, and stared at the telephone. I checked my watch. Eleven o'clock. That meant it was ten o'clock at my mother's townhouse in Dallas.

My Texas grandmother always told me not

148

to call anyone before nine a.m. or after nine p.m. It was an absolute of Texas etiquette. I felt relieved. I could postpone calling my mom until the next day. Feeling smug, I collected my pajamas and went back downstairs to the bathroom for a shower. I wasn't a chicken. I was simply being polite, or so I told myself.

The next morning the *Grand Rapids Press* was full of the strange death of a retired sheriff in a Warner County retirement center. The current sheriff, Miles DeBoer Smith, said he was conferring with the Michigan State Police, which I knew was routine in rural counties. Neither Smith nor the state police spokesman had said much to the newspaper. They barely confirmed that Van Hoosier was dead, but the reporter had found out about the signs of a struggle in Van Hoosier's room.

"Controversial" was the adjective the *Press* used to describe Van Hoosier's career in office. The rest of the story was pretty factual.

Van Hoosier had been born in Warner County and had attended public schools in Dorinda. "Boasts that his humble beginnings gave him an affinity for the working man were always part of his campaign rhetoric," the *Press* article said.

149

But Van Hoosier was apparently the last of his humble family. "Van Hoosier never married," the article said, "Acquaintances said they knew of no close relatives."

Van Hoosier apparently hadn't gone to college. He served in Korea with the U.S. Army, and after his discharge was a deputy for a previous sheriff until he ran for the office himself. He held the office twenty years.

The newspaper report then said something I found really interesting: "Van Hoosier left office at the age of fifty-two. Since that time he had divided his time between a home in Dorinda and a houseboat he kept on the Florida Intracoastal Waterway. His boat won a national prize for interior design three years ago."

The old guy had retired at fifty-two? And he'd had a house in Dorinda plus a houseboat on the Intracoastal Waterway? A houseboat that won a prize for interior design?

It sounded to me as if serving as a county official in Warner County, Michigan, had turned out to be pretty profitable for Carl Van Hoosier. Especially coming from those "humble beginnings."

"Van Hoosier suffered a stroke last summer while staying in Dorinda. He subsequently moved to the Dorinda retirement center," the article concluded.

I thought about the article as I got ready for work. I made several deductions. First, Carl Van Hoosier hadn't been a very nice guy. I'd already decided that from what Mercy Woodyard had said, of course, but reading between the lines of the article on his death certainly confirmed it. The newspaper hadn't interviewed his "friends," for example. "Acquaintances" had been the best they could come up with.

Second, Van Hoosier had apparently used the sheriff's office to make a lot of money. When a guy who came from "humble beginnings" and who had no family to will him property winds up living in a prize-winning houseboat on a Florida waterway in the winter and spending the summer near the shore of Lake Michigan, he didn't do it by saving his loose change in a pickle jar. I was willing to bet the McKays weren't the only summer people he'd done favors for.

But his story had a pitiful end. Inez had implied that his fellow residents at the retirement center hadn't liked him, and the *Press* hadn't even found a friend to talk about him. And he'd had no family. He died alone.

Except for someone who hated him enough to kill him.

I gave a shudder, then looked at my watch.

It was eight a.m. in Dallas. Time to call my mother. The no-calls-before-nine-a.m. rule didn't function if the callee would be up getting ready for work.

I got my mom's answering machine, of course. But when I said, "Hey, Mom, it's Lee," she picked up.

"This better be an emergency," she said. "I'm late getting to the office, as usual."

She was making me feel intimidated, so I plunged into conversation. "I just wanted to tell you that the shepherd was killed yesterday." When my comment was greeted with blank silence, I figured out what I'd said.

"Sheriff!" I said. "Joe and I found Carl Van Hoosegow — I mean, Van Hoosier! We found him dead."

My mother was kind enough to ignore my tongue problems. "It couldn't happen to a nicer guy. But you said he was killed. What happened to him?"

I sketched the circumstances. "So they're not saying until there's an autopsy, but it sure sounds as if he was hit in the head, then strangled or smothered."

Mom's voice was sharp. "Why were you and Joe going to see him?"

"We were being nosy," I said.

"What made you even get interested in the jerk?"

I didn't bother to keep the resentment out of my voice. "When you mentioned him, and I found out — not from *you* — that you'd left Warner Pier on what would have been your wedding day, I got sort of curious."

"Don't tell me that situation's still a hot item in Warner Pier."

"Of course it is. You never told anybody why you left, so they're still wondering. If you'd told them, they probably would have forgotten the whole thing."

"It wasn't any of their business!"

"I'm sure that's true, but that doesn't make any diffidence. I mean, difference! They still want to know."

"And so do you."

"Yes, you're right. You're my mother, and I have a certain interest in what went on in your life before I knew you."

Mom sighed deeply. "I can't blame you, I guess. But it was just so humiliating."

"You were embarrassed?"

"No! Humiliated. This wasn't a matter of my slip showing or getting caught necking — or even something more. The whole episode was *deeply* humiliating. I didn't feel that I could ever face anyone from Warner Pier again."

"Do you still feel that way?"

"Well, after I found out that Bill had committed suicide, I didn't feel that way anymore. But — remember, I was still a teenager — at the time I just didn't think I could bear it."

"Bear what? Why *did* you leave?"

Mom took a deep breath, and her next words came out in a rush.

"I left because my fiancé took me to South Haven and put me on a bus. He told me to get out of town. But he never told me why."

CHAPTER 11

Along silence followed that one. I was too astonished to reply, and I guess my mom had said all she wanted to say.

I finally spoke, but I didn't say anything original. "Bill Dykstra *asked* you to leave Warner Pier?"

"That's what I said."

"But he didn't tell you why?"

"That's what I said, Lee!"

"I heard it, I simply can't absorb it." I thought again before I came up with a question. "Did he tell you he was going to commit suicide?"

"He didn't tell me anything. We went out after the rehearsal dinner, and we were — planning to go out for a while afterward. But Bill suddenly switched directions, brought me home and told me to get my suitcase. Then he took me down to South Haven." Mom took a deep breath that almost sounded like a sob. "He gave me money — I guess all the money he had, money he'd put together for our honeymoon. He dumped me at an all-night gas station."

"Not the bus station?"

"The bus station wasn't open. I had to wait until six a.m., then take a cab there. The bus station was at a downtown bookstore in those days."

My mom had been barely eighteen years old. Her fiancé had insisted on driving her to a strange town, dumped her out on the highway at an all-night gas station, and told her to go to one of the largest cities in the United States. Alone. I thought about it before I spoke again.

"You must have been terrified," I said.

A gulp came from the other end of the line. Now I was sure Mom was crying.

"It was awful," she said. "It's a miracle I wasn't picked up by white slavers or something else terrible. Bill kept telling me I must do *exactly* what he said. 'It's for your safety,' he said. 'You'll be in danger.' "

"In danger of what?"

"He wouldn't tell me! I've never known."

"Did he say he'd get in touch with you?"

"I was supposed to go to the hotel where we'd stayed on our senior trip. He said he'd call the next night. But he didn't!"

The last sentence was almost a wail. Then I heard a soft click. Mom had hung up.

I broke the connection, then punched the redial button. I got the answering machine again and yelled. "It's me, Mom. Talk to me!" But this time she didn't pick up.

I hung up and sat there staring out the window, looking at the snowy Michigan landscape. Then I punched redial again.

"Mom," I told the answering machine. "I'm coming to Dallas. I'll call as soon as I get a flight."

"No!" I realized my mom had picked up the phone. "No! Don't come."

"But we need to talk this out face-to-face."

"Yes, you're right. But I've got some free miles. I'll clear my calendar and fly to Grand Rapids. We can talk." She gave an unconvincing laugh. "Maybe we can talk about something more pleasant than my past. I need a few days off. Maybe we can even have some fun. I can have a little input on your wedding, whether you want it or not. I'll call you as soon as I have an arrival time."

I drove to work with my head in a spin. My mother was coming to Warner Pier — and not just for a funeral, wedding, or other ceremony. She was actually coming to see me.

Weird.

Aunt Nettie was as astonished by the news as I was, but she was as practical as ever. "I hope she doesn't come today," she said. "We'll have to clear out the guest room tonight."

Like most guest rooms, Aunt Nettie's collected things that were tidied away out of other rooms in the house. Right at the moment the bed was piled with wedding notebooks, magazines, and lists, and the closet was full of summer clothes.

"I'll straighten the room tonight," I said. "I don't see how Mom can get here before tomorrow or Saturday."

"What will we feed her?" The menu is always a major concern for Aunt Nettie, since she's a real foodie.

"I'll think about it and shop this afternoon," I said. "This ought to be a slow day retailwise."

Ha. That was the day the entire population of Warner Pier lined up and marched to our front door. People who had never been near the place before picked that day to become customers.

A lot of them were like my pal Lindy. She came in because she'd read the paper and wanted to know how Joe and I happened to stumble over the body of former sheriff Carl Van Hoosier. I didn't mind talking to Lindy, of course, but I dodged everyone else's questions. Politely, or so I hoped. Most of them felt obligated to buy a few chocolates. I sold chocolate to Thomas Hilton, who owned the Garden Shop; to Barbara, the bank manager; to Diane Denham, who runs a B and B. Of course, Diane was an established customer, though she did more business with us in the summer, when her B and B was usually full of guests. It seemed as if a dozen others came in as well, and the phone rang and rang.

At least Rollie Taylor had no questions. He showed up around ten a.m. and said he needed to buy a pound of chocolates as a gift for the city clerk. As I said, some of the new customers had really dumb excuses, and I considered this one of them. The relationship between the city clerk and the city councilmen ought to be purely business. I didn't think it should include chocolates.

I also didn't think tightwad Rollie would have any idea how much a pound of Ten-Huis chocolates costs. When I mentioned the cost, he looked a little pale. A half pound would do, he said.

"Have you been causing Pat extra work?" I said. "I wouldn't think she would expect gifts from the councilmen."

"Pat looked some things up for me," Rollie said. "And, of course, I wanted to come in and check on you. How are you doing? Right after you and Joe found Van Hoosier yesterday, you seemed to be pretty shaken."

"Since it wasn't the body of anyone I knew, it wasn't too bad a shirt. I mean, shock! How do you want these chocolates? Assorted flavors? Part solid chocolate?"

Rollie blinked. "Not too many hard centers," he said.

I realized that Rollie didn't even know what kind of chocolate we made. "I'll make up a variety box," I said.

"That sounds fine. And, Lee, did you know that if Bo Derek married Don Ho, she'd be Bo Ho?"

I groaned and reached for an empty box. "I'm happy to say I didn't, Rollie. I also didn't know you did that much volunteer work at the Pleasant Creek Center. I guess that former sheriff wasn't a stranger to you."

Rollie spoke sharply. "What do you mean by that?"

I stared at him. In spite of the brusque tone to his question, he was smiling his usual smile. Had my question upset him?

"You said he was one of your bingo regulars."

"Oh! That!" There was no mistaking the relief in Rollie's voice. "I can't say I knew Van Hoosier any better than the other bingo players. I just call the numbers and hand out the prizes." Then he leaned on the counter, very casually. "But if you didn't know the old guy, why did you and Joe go over to see him?"

Rollie had talked to Joe a few minutes after we found Van Hoosier dead. But I didn't know what Joe had told him. So I waffled.

"I thought you asked Joe about that."

"I did, and he told me about finding him. But he didn't explain why the two of you had gone there in the first place."

So it was up to me. I'd already made up an answer to that question that wasn't exactly a lie, so I trotted it out with all the aplomb I could muster. "Like I said at the council meeting, I've been doing a little historical rescue. I mean, research! I had a couple of questions to ask him."

"Historical research? What for?"

"It's going to be a surprise. I'd appreciate your not mentioning it." I held the box out. "Do you think Pat would like some Jamaican rum truffles? They're dark outside over a dark interior."

"Who could resist?" Rollie's grin looked more real at the thought. "Has your mom decided when she's coming up for the wedding?"

"Not exactly, Rollie. Hey! I haven't offered you a sample. Pick something."

It's easy to distract people when you have a whole counter full of chocolate to use for that purpose. Rollie selected a double-fudge bonbon ("layers of milk and dark chocolate fudge with a dark chocolate coating"), and I was able to collect the cash for Pat's chocolates, then ease him out the door without telling him my mother was due in Warner Pier anytime now.

I didn't have the same luck a little later. The shop was empty for the first time in an hour when the phone rang a few minutes before twelve. I took the call in my office.

"Lee, it's Mom. I got a flight to Grand Rapids on Saturday."

"Let me find a pencil." I scrabbled through the piles on my desk and found pencil and paper, then took down the information. "Three thirty Saturday. I'll be there."

"Oh, no. I'll rent a car."

"Mom, there's no point in your spending money on a rental car."

"I don't want you to have to haul me around."

"But we've got loads of cars here. Aunt Nettie doesn't put five thousand miles a year on her Buick. I have my van. There's Joe's truck. You can use either the Buick or the van anytime."

"Thanks, but no thanks. I got a really good deal on a car."

"Mom! I'll meet you!" This was a bone my mom and I had chewed over hundreds of times. She was always broke, with credit card debt out the kazoo, because of these "good deals" she simply couldn't turn down. "You don't need to spend money on a rental car!"

"Lee, don't lecture me about how I spend my money."

I ground my teeth and resisted the temptation to tell her I wouldn't be counting on an inheritance from her; she'd be lucky to leave enough to pay off her MasterCard. I merely repeated her arrival information back, ending up with, "And we'll watch for a rental car to pull into the drive a little after five."

Mom and I exchanged good-byes, and I hung up.

Then a voice sounded, practically beside me. It had a gloating sound.

163

"Ha! So your mom is coming up to help with the wedding plans. Won't her Warner Pier friends be pleased?"

Greg Glossop was standing in the door to my office.

My heart plummeted to my knees. Greg Glossop — known to Warner Pier locals as Greg Gossip — had the biggest mouth on the east shore of Lake Michigan. And as the druggist at the pharmacy in the town's only supermarket, he was in a position to get the scoop on everything that went on in Warner Pier. I wouldn't go so far as accusing Greg of blabbing about his customer's private prescriptions, but he sat up in an elevated area and watched everybody who came and went at the Superette. He had also been known to climb down from his aerie and ask nosy questions. He knew who came in with whom and how long they would be in Warner Pier; who bought extra steaks and whom they had invited over for dinner; and who lingered in the baby food aisle and which of their kids was coming home for the weekend and bringing grandchildren.

I tried to stay on friendly terms with Greg. For one thing, I'm nearly as nosy as he is. Sometimes I want information about people, and it's easy to pump Greg for it. And for a second thing, I didn't want to be the victim of his tongue; I want to be on his good side.

So I resisted the temptation to kick Greg in the kneecap. "Yes, Mom's got a few days off," I said. "But we wanted to have a quiet visit, Greg. I'd appreciate it if you didn't tell all her old friends that she'll be around. She won't have time to see too many people."

Greg smiled all over his round face. That face, plus his thin hair, make him look as if he has more skin than normal. He rubbed his plump hands together and bounced on his toes, an action that made his belly resemble a basketball.

"Oh, I won't say a word, Lee."

Like I believed that.

But Greg was still talking. "I really came in to say I'm so sorry you and Joe had that terrible experience yesterday."

He dithered on for five or ten minutes, first hinting and then almost demanding that I tell him all the gory details about finding Van Hoosier. I gave him a raspberry cream bonbon ("red raspberry puree in white chocolate interior, encased in a dark chocolate"), but no more information than he would have read in the *Grand Rapids Press*. And the darn guy didn't even buy anything.

But Greg didn't leave either. So I fell back

on a technique I'd used on Greg Glossop in the past. I began to ask *him* questions.

"I guess you knew Sheriff Van Hoosier," I said.

"Why do you say that?"

"You know pretty much everybody in Warner County, Greg. He seems to have been a controversial character. What did you think of him?"

The effect of this question was amazing. Greg Glossop began to stutter and stammer and edge toward the door.

"Oh, I didn't know him. He was, he was . . . he didn't get over on this side of the county very much."

"But, Greg, he apparently left office under quite a cloud. Do you know what all that was about?"

"I was just a kid, Lee. I was working as a sacker at the Superette the year he resigned." Greg was still edging toward the door.

"But people were mad at him. Surely you heard something."

"All I heard was from Dick — Dick Van Heisel. He owned the Superette in those days. He called Van Hoosier because some guy was doing drug deals in the Superette parking lot."

That made sense. The newspapers for that

summer had had a lot of letters to the editor about drug activity. I nodded encouragingly.

"Well, Dick was sure that Van Hoosier had covered up something about drug activities in the county."

"What?"

"How would I know?" Greg Glossop looked horrified. "I have no idea. I was just a kid!"

Now he didn't edge toward the door. He threw it open and plunged out. And he plunged right into Jason Foster, who'd been in the process of opening the door to the shop.

It took Jason and Greg a minute to get untangled, apologize, and say hello and good-bye to each other. So I had a minute to absorb Greg's words and the way he'd said them.

Greg had been his usual gossipy self until I asked him for his own opinion about Sheriff Carl Van Hoosier. Then he'd begun to hem and haw. He hadn't wanted to say anything. Finally he'd come up with the name of someone else who had been upset with Van Hoosier. That had seemed to relieve him. He had quickly tried to focus my attention on the former owner of the Superette — a man who was probably dead now, twenty-five years after the events in question. Then Greg had dashed for the door so quickly that he almost bowled Jason over.

By the time I'd analyzed this, Jason was inside the shop, and I tried to put the episode with Greg aside. Jason was an old friend. I prepared my spiel about finding a dead body and my assurances that I was going to survive the experience.

Jason strode over to the counter and spoke.

"Sorry it took me so long to get back to you," he said.

His remark left me feeling completely blank. "Back to me?"

"Yes. You called yesterday. What did you need?"

CHAPTER 12

I couldn't imagine what he was talking about. At that moment, my phone call to Jason might have been made in another lifetime, instead of just twenty-four hours earlier. I scrambled to remember it.

"Oh!" I said. "I'd forgiven — I mean, forgotten! I mean . . ." Then the fog cleared. Jason had been a bearer at Bill Dykstra's funeral. I'd planned to ask him about Bill.

"Come in the office," I said. "I'll get someone to watch the counter, and we can talk."

I gave Jason a chocolate I knew was his favorite — Italian cherry ("an oval bonbon with a dark chocolate shell, filled with white chocolate flavored with Amarena cherry"). He sat in my visitor's chair while I ran to ask Dolly Jolly to keep an eye the counter. Then I sat in my own chair and stared at Jason. I wasn't sure just how to begin.

Jason licked cherry filling off his lips and

looked at me with raised eyebrows. "Why did you call, Lee?"

A direct question seemed to be the simplest way to answer his direct question. "Jason," I said, "how well did you know Bill Dykstra?"

"Bill? God, I haven't thought of Bill in a million years. That was a real tragedy." Jason sighed deeply. "I met Bill when we were both attending technical school in Holland. He was in electronics, and I was in food service, but we served on the student council together. He tipped me off to the first job I landed down here, so in a way Bill's the reason I wound up in Warner Pier. I even stayed with his family the first couple of months I worked here."

"Then you knew the whole family well."

"I only met Ed — the brother — once. That was the first year Bill and I were in school together." Then Jason frowned. "But don't get it wrong. Bill and I were just friends. I was still way inside the closet back then. He had no idea. . . . How'd you find out that I knew him?"

"I looked up his obituary, and you were a bearer. What kind of a guy was he?"

Jason stared at the ceiling a minute. "I always thought he was a lot like his dad. Uncomplicated. Liked to work with his hands. Maybe more interested in how things worked than in how people worked."

"Were you surprised by his suicide?"

"Surprised isn't the word for it. Try stunned. Or totally freakin' amazed. I'd been at the rehearsal dinner on Friday night, and he seemed completely happy. Nervous, of course, and excited. But pleased. Then Saturday morning his dad called to say the wedding was apparently off and Bill was missing. I helped hunt for Bill. But I'm glad to say I wasn't the one who found him."

"Do you have any idea why Bill called the wedding off?"

Jason's eyes widened. "I didn't know he did. We all thought that was Sally's idea."

"Mom says not."

"She didn't figure out that he was suicidal? Decide he wasn't a good marriage risk? That's what I always figured happened."

"No, Mom says Bill was the one who backed out. And she says he wouldn't explain why. He put her on the bus, made her leave town."

"Good night!" Jason shook his head. "I always thought Bill was the sane person in his family, but maybe he was as nutty as the rest of them."

"Were they all peculiar? Of course, Lovie

. . ." Jason and I both raised our eyebrows. "But I didn't know that the father and the other brother were odd, too."

"They weren't nutty, really. In fact, they were nice people in a lot of ways."

Jason thought a few moments before he spoke again. "I guess the Dykstras were an example of what the sixties and seventies were all about. Ed Sr. was a blue-collar guy, an electrician and general handyman. He could build anything, repair anything. World War II vet. High school education. Fishing trips and beer at the corner bar type. Then — I got this from things Bill told me — when the boys were little, their mom decided she needed to work."

I nodded. "Reflecting the social changes of the era. Women's rights."

"I don't know about that. I think they needed the money. Maybe that's the same thing. Anyway, Mrs. Dykstra had always been a more intellectual type than Ed Sr. She decided to go to college so she could get a job as a teacher, which was one of the better jobs for women at the time. But in college, she got into the ecology group, began to work hard to save the environment. Which sounds great, except that Mr. Dykstra thought all those people were a bunch of pinkos, so he didn't like her going to demonstrations and such. Then Ed Jr., who was really into Scouting, began working on his Eagle, and Mrs. Dykstra helped him come up with some environmental project. So Ed Jr. wound up in the save-the-environment movement and began protesting with his mom. After he went to Ann Arbor, that protesting led him into the antiwar movement. He dropped out of college, which made him eligible for the draft. So he went to Canada. Which their dad really thought was pinko."

"How did Bill feel about all this?"

"Caught in the middle. Mostly, he sided with his dad, because he and his dad had always looked at the world in the same way. Or maybe it was because he thought Ed Jr. was siding with their mom. Or their mom was siding with Ed Jr. Judging from what Bill used to say, their home life went right down the tube. I think that's why Bill went to electronics school, instead of college. He wanted to get out on his own as fast as possible."

"Probably that's why he wanted to get married, too."

"That may have been part of it, Lee. But he was nuts about your — about Sally. Anyway, I saved my tips and bought a suit at JCPenney to wear in the wedding. And I had to wear it for the funeral instead."

"I was surprised to see that Rollie Taylor was a bearer, too. How did he know Bill?"

"I don't think he did, really. He was called in at the last minute. He was a friend of Bill's mom."

"Of Lovie's?"

"Yeah. We didn't call her Lovie then. I guess she'll always be Mrs. Dykstra to me. But she had known Rollie over at Western Michigan. They took education classes together. I know she urged him to apply for a job over here."

"Did Bill have a problem with drinking?"

"No! Whatever gave you that idea? If the guys went out, he — well, nowadays we would have said he was the designated driver. He rarely drank at all. I was amazed when I heard there were beer cans in his car when they found him."

"How about drugs? Pot?"

"Lee, you've been listening to too much hearsay about our generation. Jokes like, 'If you can remember the sixties and seventies, you weren't there.' Very funny. And it may have been true for a lot of people. But if Bill had a weakness, it was for chocolate. He would have killed for a homemade brownie. Maybe he was marrying Sally because he wanted to cozy up to her brother the chocolatier."

Jason laughed, then went on. "Bill and I were worker bees. The draft had been abolished, so we didn't have to worry about getting killed in Vietnam. We were trying to get jobs and keep them, get on with our lives. We weren't out smoking pot every night. And neither was your mom."

"But the sheriff found pot in Bill's car. After he was dead."

Jason let that soak in for a moment. Then he seemed to go nuts. He jumped to his feet. He twisted his body as if he were in pain. He clenched his fists in the air. He yanked at his ponytail.

He obviously wanted to walk up and down, maybe kick something, but there was nothing kickable in my office, and there was no pacing room.

I didn't know if I should panic or not. I'd been around Jason when half his waiters didn't show up, when the chef ruined the steamboat round, and when the bartender got drunk and passed out behind the bar. But I'd never before seen him go berserk. He seemed to be completely incoherent. I considered calling 9-1-1. My report about Bill Dykstra had almost sent Jason over the edge.

Finally Jason leaned across my desk, putting his face close to mine. He pounded a fist on my blotter.

"No!" he said. "Bill never used pot! You're lying!"

"It's not *my* story, Jason! A law enforcement official told Joe and me that. Someone who saw the sheriff's reports at the time."

"Then he lied!"

I began to wonder if Mac McKay had been wrong. Had he remembered incorrectly? I tried to soothe Jason. "Well, naturally, the guy who told us that could be wrong."

"I suppose it was your pal Hogan Jones!"

"No, Hogan . . ." I tried to tell him Chief Jones hadn't even been in Warner Pier thirty-three years earlier, but Jason was talking again.

"No! Jones hasn't been there that long! It must have been that jerk Van Hoosier himself! That old liar! I'll find him and kick him in the patootie!"

"You're too late," I said. "Somebody kicked him yesterday. Permanently."

"What do you mean?"

I picked up my copy of the *Grand Rapids Press* and pointed to the news story on Van Hoosier's death. Jason read it rapidly.

Jason threw the newspaper down and said exactly what my mom had said. "It couldn't

176

happen to a nicer guy."

He looked at me sharply. "But if you and Joe didn't talk to Van Hoosier, who told you that pot was found in Bill's car?"

I decided it wouldn't be wise to give Mac McKay's name to Jason in his present mood.

"A guy who worked with Van Hoosier told us," I said. "And his opinion of Van Hoosier was exactly the same as yours, incidentally. Plus, he didn't have the original report in front of him. It may not even still be in existence. So we can't check it out. But why are you so sure that Bill didn't smoke pot?"

"Bill hated that stuff. He'd seen what it did to his brother. Bill was really disgusted with him. Ed quarreled with their dad over his antiwar viewpoint, but their mom always took Ed's side. Then she figured out he was doing drugs and kicked him out."

"So Ed didn't simply run away to Canada. He was booted out of the family home."

"Something like that. And I guess he didn't come home, even after his dad died and even after Jimmy Carter gave the guys who split for Canada a get-out-of-jail card. Ed might have contacted his mother, of course. None of us would be likely to ask her if she'd heard from him."

I trotted out the rest of the names from

Bill Dykstra's obituary, asking Jason if they were close friends of Bill's. He confirmed that the first three guys had left Warner Pier.

"That was a long time ago," Jason said. "Bill and Tom Hilton were high school buddies. But why are you looking for friends of Bill's, anyway?"

He had me there. I'd started the search because I wanted to know why my mom had fled Warner Pier on her wedding day, and she hadn't seemed inclined to tell me. But now Mom was headed to Michigan, and she'd promised to talk to me. Tell all. So I really had no excuse for quizzing people about Bill Dykstra.

All this ran through my mind while Jason sat in my visitor's chair and looked at me expectantly. I had to say something, no matter how stupid it sounded.

"I'm just curlicue," I said. "I mean, curious! My mom never told me about all of this, and I wanted to know. Actually, last night she agreed to tell me — her side, at least."

I told Jason about my mom's forthcoming visit, again issuing a warning that she'd be here only a short time. I didn't know that she'd want to see Jason, or that he'd want to see her, but that gave both of them an out.

Jason went into another round of questions then, which I luckily recognized as an attempt to learn who had told Joe and me about the pot found in the car with Bill Dykstra. I was able to head him off, but I vowed to call Joe ASAP and tell him that Jason was after our informant with blood in his eye. Not that I thought Jason would actually attack Mac McKay. But he might bad-mouth him, and I'd rather he didn't do it by name. Actually, as long as any confrontation between Jason and Mac remained verbal, I felt sure that Mac could hold his own.

Jason left, and I was reaching for the telephone, ready to punch the key on the speed dial that would summon Joe to the other end of the line, when — once again — the door to the shop opened.

I looked up to see a tall man coming in. He was dressed for the Michigan winter — shrouded in a parka zipped up over his chin and a stocking cap pulled down over his ears. Only a sliver of his face was visible, a sliver that featured a distinctive broad nose.

A stranger. Maybe he was a legitimate customer. I took my place behind the counter. "May I help you?"

"I need a box of chocolates." His voice was unusually raspy. I wondered if he was

179

getting over a cold. "A pound, I guess."

I immediately told him the price. I didn't want the bill to surprise him. Unlike Rollie, the newcomer didn't turn pale. He nodded, agreeing to cough up a nice stack of bills. Next I asked him if he wanted specific chocolates. He looked blank. Obviously, I had another customer who didn't know what TenHuis manufactured. I handed him a list of flavors and gave him a guided tour of the showcases, pointing out the decorations of each flavor.

"Plus you get to pick a free sample," I added. "What sounds good to you?"

The tall man picked a Frangelico truffle ("hazelnut interior coated in milk chocolate"). Just a bit venturesome, and really good. I gave him one, and he moved to the window — truffle in one hand, list of flavors in the other.

The door opened again, but the person who came in this time was no stranger. It was Mike Herrera, the mayor of Warner Pier.

I hid my sigh and greeted him. Mike's one of my favorite people, but I needed to work, not talk. Besides, in the battle over who was going to pay for the wedding reception, Mike was dating Joe's mom, so he was naturally on Mercy's side. And since he was the owner of the restaurant where we were having the reception, he was in a position to swing a lot of weight.

Not that I minded getting a nice discount. But we didn't want Mercy to run the reception, and we didn't want to feel that we were indebted to Mike for giving us an extra-special price. We wanted to pay our own way and pick out our own menu.

Mike glanced at the man in the heavy jacket. Mike's a merchant, and I knew he would never keep me from waiting on a customer. But he apparently could tell that the man was thinking about his purchase, so he walked over to the counter and pulled off his hat, a sort of furry fedora.

"How're y'all?" he said.

Mike is a fellow Texan, one of the few I've found in western Michigan, and he makes sure he hangs onto his "y'all." Since he knew "y'all" is the plural form of "you," I knew he was asking about Aunt Nettie as well as me.

"Aunt Nettie and I are doing fine, Mike. What can I do for you?"

"I figured out what I wanted to geef you and Joe as a wedding present."

Uh-oh. Mike's Tex-Mex accent was coming out. That meant he felt nervous. What was he up to?

"We don't really expect anything, Mike. Of course, a place setting of our stainless would be nice."

"No. I'm gonna geef you and Joe champagne."

"We'd love a bottle."

"How many people are coming to the reception?"

"Oh." As I suspected, Mike had joined Mercy's campaign to pay for — and run — the reception.

Mike leaned closer. "How many? A hundred? Two hundred?"

"Right now we've got twelve."

"Twelve hundred people!" Mike looked very surprised.

"No, Mike. Twelve people. You, Mercy, Aunt Nettie, Hogan, Lindy, Tony, my dad, my stepmother, my stepsister, my mother, and Joe and me. Plus the minister. Thirteen."

Mike rolled his eyes.

The tall man had turned around, and I spoke to him. "Have you decided, sir? Do you want specific flavors or just a sampler?"

"One of each?" He sounded like a badly tuned bullfrog.

"That will make a half-pound box."

"Then I guess I need two of each."

"Great." I folded a box, lined it with paper

and began filling it. Mike leaned over the counter and spoke in a low voice. "Mercy would like to pay for the whole reception."

"I know, Mike. She told Joe and me that. But I'm going to hang on to the etiquette books on this one. It's the bride's side of the wedding party that's supposed to pay for the reception. So I don't want Mercy to get involved. I'll handle the reception. And that includes buying the champagne."

"Mercy —"

"Mike! My dad sent a check to help. I appreciate Mercy's offer, but I'd rather handle it myself."

My dad's check wouldn't pay for a quarter of the reception, of course. I was pretty sure that Mike knew my father's circumstances were modest. He'd guess the truth.

I kept loading the box, and I concentrated on the paying customer again, trying to be friendly. "Has it gotten colder out?"

The tall man ducked his head and croaked out an answer. "It hasn't warmed up." He seemed to begrudge every word I dug out of him. Not a friendly type. In fact, he turned his back on me and went over to stare out the window again. All three of us were silent while I finished filling the box and tying its blue ribbon neatly.

"Here you go, sir," I said.

Mike shuffled his feet, plainly waiting to begin arguing again while I made change for the hundred-dollar bill the man in the stocking cap handed me.

"Thanks." His final word was as gruff as the rest of his conversation.

Mike stared at him as he went out the door. "He sure looks like . . ." His voice trailed off, and he turned back to me. "Now listen, Lee, I've made my mind up. I'm giving you and Joe the champagne for the reception as a wedding gift, and it's gonna be good champagne, not cheap stuff. I don't want to hear another word about it. All you can do is say thank-you like a Texas lady."

He jammed his furry hat on his head. Then he left, walking like a man who knows his own mind.

I ran to the door and put my head out. "Mike!" I said. He didn't turn around.

"Thanks, Mike! But, no thanks!"

The battle over the reception was beginning to wear me down.

CHOCOLATE CHAT:
CHILDHOOD CHOCOLATE — PART II

My husband, David Sandstrom, grew up in the big city, in the Riverdale section of the Bronx.

Right near the Fanny Farmer chocolate factory.

Talk about bliss.

"My biggest chocolate memory," he says, "is walking down the hill to the subway station and passing within two blocks of the Fanny Farmer factory. When the wind was from the north — wow! You didn't care what kind of chocolate it was — soft-center, hard-center, or caramel — if you could just smell Fanny Farmer."

Dave also remembers with zest the machine on the subway platform that dispensed a tiny Hershey's bar. For a penny.

Talk about the good old days.

— *JoAnna Carl*

CHAPTER 13

Joe called then and asked me to meet him for lunch. I dumped the responsibility for TenHuis Chocolade's retail sales on Dolly Jolly and left. I was tired of answering questions. Joe already knew how we'd happened to stumble across a dead body the previous afternoon, and he had a pretty good idea of how I felt about it, so we could talk about something different.

Unless he'd managed to ask Rollie about Bill Dykstra. But he hadn't done that yet, Joe told me. I was relieved.

After an hour of talking with Joe about topics such as Mike Herrera insisting on buying champagne for our reception, I felt refreshed and reenergized and headed back to work. And I did work. The phone did not ring, the front door did not open, and I accomplished quite a bit.

By four thirty, when the front door did open again, I was feeling triumphant. I looked up to see a stranger, the second stranger who'd been in that day. This one was also shrouded in Michigan winter wear, although instead of a stocking cap he had the hood of his parka pulled down over his face.

I got up and went to the counter. "May I help you?"

"Hi, Ms. McKinney," the man said. He shoved the hood back and revealed a completely bald head.

Then I did know him. It was Elmer Priddy, RN, the man who had confirmed the death of Carl Van Hoosier twenty-four hours earlier.

"Hello! I didn't expect to see you again."

"I heard you tell the deputy you worked here. I get over to Warner Pier on my days off. Look at an art gallery, eat in a good restaurant. Get a little culture with a capital K."

"You'll have to include chocolate." I gestured at the display counter. "Pick a sample."

This called for a bit of discussion, of course. I defy anyone to simply pick a Ten-Huis bonbon or truffle without debating between the round coconut-covered one and the dark chocolate square with one dot of milk chocolate in the center. But after a couple of minutes Priddy was munching a dark chocolate square, known to TenHuis fans as a lemon canache bonbon ("tangy lemon interior with dark chocolate coating"). Canache — pronounced "ca-nosh" — is a type of filling, sort of a soft jelly. We don't make hard-jellied centers.

As Priddy rolled his eyes in bliss, I brought up the unpleasant events of the previous afternoon. "I don't suppose there's an official report on what killed Van Hoosier."

"Not yet."

"Joe and I were a little surprised that you agreed with him about Van Hoosier's death being suspicious."

"Your fiancé identified the main thing right away. The red dots in the conjunctivae, the inside of the eyelid. It's hard to miss. And Van Hoosier had that lump on the side of his head; I could tell that easily. So when the doctor agreed . . ." He shrugged.

"Did the blow kill him?"

"Oh, no. In fact" — he leaned across the counter — "there was a pillow — I think the killer tried to smother him, but Van Hoosier was feistier than he'd expected. When he fought back, the killer must have hit him. Stunned him. Then used the pillow."

I shuddered. "Van Hoosier doesn't sound

like he was a very nice man, but that's awful! Do the police have any suspects?"

"They wouldn't be telling me. But dozens of people go up and down that hall every day. Residents, staff, visitors — heck, the florist comes by. And the dry cleaner."

"Do you have any idea how long he'd been dead?"

"That's for the experts to figure out. But the doctor took his temp, and judging by that, I'd guess at least two hours."

I gave a chuckle that didn't sound funny even to me. "I guess that clears Joe and me then. We'd only been at Pleasant Creek an hour."

Priddy's chuckle sounded genuinely amused. "And you didn't have any motive for killing him, right?"

"None at all. In fact, we wanted to meet him, and he died before we got a chance." Then I added quickly. "Not that there could be any conjunction. I mean, connection!"

Priddy was nice enough to ignore my twisted tongue. "You didn't know him at all?"

"No, I'd only heard of him."

"That's odd." The bald man looked puzzled.

"Why?"

He leaned across the counter, frowning.

"This is TenHuis Chocolade, right?"

"Yes."

"But your name is Lee McKinney. Is there a TenHuis in the business?"

"My Aunt Nettie." I reached into the counter and, using the tiny tongs we use to serve chocolates, I began to neaten up the rows of mocha pyramids. "Actually, she's Jeannette TenHuis. But she's a TenHuis by marriage, not birth."

Priddy looked more puzzled. "Is there a Sally TenHuis?"

I jumped so hard my tongs sent a couple of pyramids flying into the glass front of the case. I know I gave Priddy a wild-eyed look.

"Sally is my motive," I said. "I mean, my mother! My mother — of course, she's Sally McKinney now — was a TenHuis. But she was never assorted — I mean, associated! She was never associated with TenHuis Chocolade. How did you hear of her?"

"Oh, Van Hoosier used to mutter about her."

"Van Hoosier! Why? What did he have to say about my mother?"

Priddy gave a major shrug. "I never could understand. He'd gotten awfully vague mentally, you know. He hadn't been diagnosed with Alzheimer's or anything. But his mind wandered."

"Did you talk to him a lot?"

"Maybe more than I talk to some of the other residents. He could get around by himself, but he took a lot of medication, and he had to be supervised. He was one of those who would pretend to swallow, then spit his pills in the trash. That wing is my responsibility five afternoons a week. Besides, Van Hoosier was lonely. He didn't have any family. He'd never married. I guess the nearest thing he had to friends was the McDonald's retiree coffee klatch, and those guys didn't exactly come around to visit all the time."

I mentally contrasted Van Hoosier with Mac McKay — Mac with his committees, close family, church friends, and comfortable home. Mac was healthier than Van Hoosier had been, of course, but the differences weren't all a matter of health. Mac would never be alone because he had invested himself in friends, family, and community while he was active. Instead of leaving his hometown for the Florida Intracoastal Waterway when he retired, he stayed around and served on the library board.

Van Hoosier apparently hadn't bothered to develop friendships. The rich people whom he'd done favors for weren't interested in Van Hoosier once he wasn't in a position to help them out.

Van Hoosier might have had a lot more money than Mac, but Mac was much richer.

That didn't explain why Van Hoosier would have talked about my mother. "I don't understand why Van Hoosier would have been interested in my mom," I said. I tried to laugh. "As far as I know she was always law-abiding."

"I don't know that he wanted to arrest her," Priddy said. "He'd just mutter her name and something about kidnapping. Was she ever kidnapped?"

"What? Absolutely not!"

Priddy shrugged again. "I just moved to Warner County ten years ago. Was there a famous kidnapping here?"

"Not that I ever heard of. There was the McKay kidnapping. The McKays have a cottage here, but the kidnapping happened in Chicago."

Priddy shrugged. "Well, like I said, Van Hoosier's mind had been wandering for as long as I'd known him."

We left it at that. Priddy stood around a few more minutes, and I asked him get-acquainted questions. Where was he from? The Detroit area, he said. How long had he worked at the Pleasant Creek Center?

Nearly a year. Did he like his job? Yes. He hadn't earned his nursing degree until he was past forty, but he found it a very rewarding profession.

Priddy bought a half-pound box of chocolates, insisting on all coffee-flavored ones — coffee truffles and mocha pyramids. Then he went out into the late afternoon gloom, leaving me confused and curious.

All these years, I gathered, my mom had feared Sheriff Van Hoosier. And all these years Van Hoosier had wondered what became of her. Maybe they should have gotten together while Van Hoosier was still alive.

But obviously Mom had gone to great lengths to avoid him. Besides, if Van Hoosier had actually wanted to find her, I told myself, he could merely have come to Uncle Phil's funeral. Or he could have come by TenHuis Chocolade. Aunt Nettie would have been willing to forward a letter to her.

Heck, since the advent of the Internet, it's easy to find anybody anywhere. Even if Van Hoosier wasn't computer literate, he could have asked the Dorinda librarian to look Mom up for him. But Van Hoosier hadn't done that. He had apparently only gotten interested in Mom at the end of his life, after his thought processes had become unclear.

And what was this about a kidnapping? I'd read all the newspapers for the year my mom ran away, and the most serious crime committed in Warner County was drug dealing. In fact, that had been a real problem when Van Hoosier was sheriff.

The only kidnappings in the news had been Patty Hearst — she'd been kidnapped a year earlier in California — and Quinn McKay. I toyed with the idea that the McKay kidnapping had some link to Warner County. But Quinn McKay had been kidnapped in Chicago and released in southern Illinois. And Aunt Nettie thought that nobody but his stepmother used the Warner Pier cottage. Quinn never came up himself.

The whole thing was nuts. I resolved to forget it until Mom arrived Saturday.

That was easy to resolve, but hard to accomplish. Warner Pier is such a small town. Even as I was resolving to forget the whole thing until Mom arrived, I glanced up and saw the Hilton Garden Shop truck go by. I could barely make the logo out in the dim light, but it reminded me that Tom Hilton had also been a bearer at Bill Dykstra's funeral. Everywhere I looked something reminded me of the questions I had about the whole situation.

I was also reminded that I had snapped at Tom Hilton the last time I talked to him. I'd been in a rush to catch the UPS man, and I hadn't wanted to discuss my mom. I hadn't taken time to be polite.

I decided to stop by the garden shop on my way home and apologize. Maybe I could ask Tom about Bill Dykstra at the same time. And I could buy Aunt Nettie a fifty-pound bag of sunflower seeds. I looked at the clock. Nearly closing time for us and for the Garden Shop. I headed out.

When I got to the shop, I found Tom standing on a ladder, arranging an elaborate display of bird feeders. He was using fishing line to hang each feeder from a frame suspended from the ceiling. The bird feeders were beautifully crafted. There was a miniature lighthouse, a Victorian mansion, a sailing boat, a fairy-tale castle. The feeders were obviously designed as yard art, rather than mere bird attractors. I wondered if Aunt Nettie's flat wooden tray wouldn't draw more birds.

Tom greeted me with a friendly grin and brushed off my apology. He smiled at me from the top of his ladder. "I understand trying to catch the UPS man," he said.

"Besides, you've got a lot to do, planning a wedding."

"We're trying to keep it small, but the thing keeps growing. I had one question for you, Tom. I just found out that you knew Bill Dykstra, the guy Mom almost married."

Tom gave me a sharp look. "What about it?"

"How did you meet him?"

"My mom took me to kindergarten, and there he was. Bill and I went through thirteen years of school together. We were in Cub Scouts together. Played basketball in high school. Worked together picking apples. I knew him my whole life, Lee."

"What did you think of him?"

"Why?" Tom asked curtly.

I told the truth. "I'm just curious, Tom. My mom never told me anything about him or about the wedding that didn't come off. And neither did anybody here in Warner Pier."

"I guess we all thought you knew."

"I suppose that's why. Anyway, I know now, and it's such a stunning part of my mom's life that I'm trying to understand how such a thing could happen."

"That's easy. Sally and Bill were young. Too young. They realized it and called the whole thing off. Sally was embarrassed and left town. End of story."

"You're leaving out Bill Dykstra's suicide."

Tom's stepped down one step on his ladder. I saw where he was looking and handed him a bird feeder that was still on the floor, this one shaped like a red barn. He hung it in place before he spoke.

"I wish I could leave Bill's suicide out," he said. "I've spent more than thirty years trying to understand it."

"Which brings me back to my original question, Tom. What kind of guy was Bill?"

Tom looked down, and this time I handed him a bird feeder shaped like an old-fashioned schoolhouse. He hung it carefully. Then he turned to me and spoke directly and firmly. "A peacemaker," he said. "Bill was a peacemaker. Even when we were little kids, he was always the one who was trying to stop fights. He would never take sides, never gang up on other kids the way boys do. He was the one who suggested taking turns. The one who was willing to share first place rather than hurt someone else's feelings."

I could see that Tom was blinking back tears, but he kept talking. "The only time I ever saw Bill mad was when some guys were making fun of another kid — bullying him. Bill waded into them. And he did the same thing when Rollie Taylor came to town."

"Rollie? But Rollie came here as a teacher."

"Right. But he was a squirrelly kind of guy in those days. Hair too long, belly too big, soft-looking. Inexperienced. He wanted to be a pal to the students, didn't keep a firm hand on discipline. So the guys in his classes gave him hell."

"Bill stood up for him?"

"Yeah. Rollie was a friend of Bill's mother. She asked Bill to look after him. Bill did. It was that simple. And Bill was popular enough that when he said to lay off Mr. Taylor, the guys laid off. Then Mrs. Dykstra took Rollie in hand, taught him the tricks of keeping an orderly classroom. Between the two of them they turned him into a pretty good teacher."

"Bill sounds like a nice guy. I bet he let Mom lead him around by the nose."

Tom laughed. "She thought she did! But when it came down to it, ol' Bill held his own. He just never raised his voice while he was doing it."

"How'd he get along with his family?"

"Ed Jr. broke his heart."

"His brother? How?"

"All that demonstrating stuff. It was all right with Lovie — Mrs. Dykstra. But Mr.

Dykstra — man, he didn't like it. It split the family."

"And Bill blamed his brother?"

"Yeah. He found out Ed had feet of clay. See, Bill had always idolized Ed. Ed protected Bill — he protected me, too. He was an Eagle Scout. He could tramp through the woods, dive from the high board at the beach, build a set of stilts, fix a bicycle, play marbles. Ed taught Bill and me all that stuff. Then Ed went off the tracks."

"I heard that Ed was even into drugs."

"I'm afraid that's right. Bill was — well, crushed — crushed by Ed's . . . rebellion. If that's the right word. Bill's idol had fallen. With a crash. Landed in Canada. Bill didn't understand how Ed could do such a thing."

"Bill didn't have sympathy for the antiwar movement?"

"Bill was a by-the-books, obey-the-rules kind of guy. If his country had called, he would have gone. And Ed had been that way, too. When we were growing up."

"Apparently both Bill and Ed changed in the way they looked at the world."

"The changes were too abrupt. At least Bill's last action was abrupt. I guess that's why I had such a hard time accepting Bill's suicide. It wasn't a by-the-rules way to act."

Tom got down from his ladder and stared

199

up at the hanging bird feeders. He seemed to consider them seriously. Then he turned to me, and I saw that he was still blinking back tears.

"I hated the idea of Bill's suicide so much that for years I tried to convince myself he had been murdered," he said.

CHAPTER 14

Murder. In all the talking I'd done about Bill Dykstra's death, this was the first time anyone had suggested it could have been anything but suicide.

But I didn't comment as I paid Tom Hilton for the birdseed or as he loaded it into the van for me. I left the garden shop. I let the idea roll around in my little brain while I started the van and moved to the exit of Tom's parking lot. I allowed it to seep in while I stopped to let a small SUV go by; I even noted that the face I saw through the side window was that of Elmer Priddy. His bald head was unmistakable with his hood pushed back for driving. And I kept Tom's idea on simmer while a ramshackle truck followed him: Lovie Dykstra with her usual load of cans. Tourists and locals: business as usual in Warner Pier. I didn't let the two vehicles interrupt my contemplation of what Tom Hilton had said.

I didn't find the idea of murder as shocking as it might have been. I'd read enough mystery novels to know that fictional murderers often tried to fake suicides. But could they do it successfully in real life?

I knew how to find out.

I headed home. Aunt Nettie had mentioned that she had invited Hogan Jones over for dinner that evening. I was going out with Joe, but I could put off our departure until after Hogan arrived. And Hogan was not only Aunt Nettie's boyfriend — if a "boy" can be in his sixties — he was also Warner Pier Police Chief. And before he'd been Warner Pier chief, he'd been a detective in the Cincinnati Police Department. He'd know if it were possible to fake a suicide and get away with it. Get away with it for thirty-three years.

I could barely wait for Hogan to get into the house so I could ask him. Luckily Aunt Nettie wasn't quite ready when his car pulled into the drive, so I was able to meet him at the door. But before I could ask him a question, he asked me one.

"You gonna be available in the morning?"

"Available? What for?"

"To make a statement about finding Van Hoosier."

"Oh. Sure. Do I have to go to Dorinda?"

"Nope. The sheriff called me at five. He tried all day to get a deputy over to take your statement. Never could manage it. So I said I'd fill in."

Hogan and I set a time for me to come by the Warner Pier PD, and I settled him into a comfortable chair in front of the fire. Then I began my interrogation.

"Hogan, can a suicide be faked? Or is that just in mystery novels?"

"Sure it can, Lee. Every experienced detective can list a dozen cases of suicide he's heard of or personally witnessed when there were a lot of unanswered questions. Why do you want to know?"

I quickly sketched the information about Bill Dykstra ordering my mom to leave Warner Pier and about the general astonishment people who had known Bill had expressed at his suicide.

Hogan shook his head in surprise at the story. But he drew the line at saying Bill Dykstra's suicide was improbable. "After a suicide, friends and relations always say they're completely amazed, Lee. None of us want to think we could have done something — listened harder, recommended counseling, been more sympathetic — and prevented a suicide."

"But it would be possible to fake a suicide

by carbon monoxide?"

"Of a young, healthy guy like you describe? It wouldn't be the easiest thing in the world. You'd have to immobilize him some way, so he didn't just get out of the car. Hit him in the head, tie him up, drug him, get him drunk."

"Wouldn't an autopsy reveal those things? I mean, blood tests would show drugs or alcohol, for example. Knocking him out would leave a lump on the back of his head."

"Yes, an autopsy could reveal the contributing cause of death. But an autopsy probably wouldn't be performed."

"No autopsy!"

Hogan shook his head. "An autopsy is done only in cases where the cause of death is unknown. If the cause of death was as obvious as a hose from the exhaust pipe to the driver's side window, it's unlikely the authorities would call for one. Of course, the family could ask for one. But that's not likely to happen."

"Why not? Wouldn't they want to know?"

"But they probably thought they did know. And autopsies cost money. A lot of money. And in that situation it would be paid by the family."

"Oh." I hadn't thought of that. "The Dykstras didn't have a lot of money, I guess."

"They were already faced with having to pay for a funeral, Lee. Unless they thought there was really something to be gained by an autopsy, they probably wouldn't have asked for one."

I thought about that until Hogan cleared his throat. "Unless," he said, "*unless* the family didn't have any confidence in the investigating officer."

That suggestion took my breath away.

Of course the Dykstras wouldn't have had any confidence in the investigating officer! The investigating officer had been that well-known crook Carl Van Hoosier!

I inhaled so abruptly that the fire in the fireplace nearly went out. "Oh! Maybe they did ask for an autopsy then!"

Hogan frowned. "The investigating officer was Sheriff Van Hoosier, I gather."

"Right! Everybody has some story about how awful he was."

"Funny how the guy got elected sheriff term after term." Hogan sat back in his chair and crossed his arms.

My jaw dropped. "I hadn't thought about that. All I hear is that he was a rotunda — I mean, rotten! Everybody says he was a rotten guy."

"Today they do. Nowadays they know he had to leave office or face malfeasance

205

charges. At the time . . ." Hogan shrugged.

"I see what you mean. The Dykstras might have trusted him, I guess. But what about the coroner?"

"You mean the medical examiner? All he does is establish the cause of death. How it happened is up to the investigating agency. And there would have been no question about what killed Bill Dykstra. Death by carbon monoxide isn't hard to diagnose. If Bill had been dead before the carbon monoxide entered the car, the ME would definitely have noticed. So I feel pretty certain Bill died of carbon monoxide poisoning."

"So there wouldn't have been a complete autopsy."

"Probably not."

I sighed deeply.

"Of course," Hogan said, "I could try to find out."

"Oh! Would you?"

"The current sheriff and I are fairly good pals. I could ask to see the records. They may be buried in a warehouse someplace, but I could ask."

I expressed my deepest gratitude, and we left it there. Aunt Nettie appeared, and in a few minutes Joe did, too. He didn't stay long enough to take off his coat. I got my jacket, and we left.

"We didn't talk about what we'd do this evening," I said after I got in his truck. "Did you have a plan?"

"I thought we'd go into Holland for dinner, but I told Rollie Taylor we'd meet him for a drink first."

I hadn't been expecting that, so I thought about it. "Have you asked him about Bill Dykstra?"

"Not yet. I called him a couple of times. He just called back a few minutes ago. This seemed to be the best way to get together with him. Is that okay with you?"

I couldn't think of any reason to object. "Sure," I said. "And let me tell you what I found out this afternoon."

I quickly sketched the comments Elmer Priddy had made, claiming Van Hoosier had linked my mom's name to a kidnapping. Joe was as surprised as I had been. Since we knew of no kidnapping that had occurred the year Mom left Warner Pier, the whole thing sounded like the ramblings of a senile mind.

Then I told Joe about Tom and his feeling that murder was a more likely scenario for Bill's death.

"I asked Hogan about it," I said, "and he said he'd look into the case."

"You realize that you might prove Bill was

murdered and make your mom suspect number one."

"Don't be silly!"

I scoffed, but the idea was chilling. I had been messing around in my mother's past — just to satisfy my own curiosity. But if I finally discovered the reason she left Warner Pier — the reason Bill Dykstra sent her away — it might turn out to be something I wished I hadn't dredged up.

I was feeling a bit nervous when Joe parked in front of the Sidewalk Café. "I see Rollie's car is already here," he said.

One reason Joe had suggested the Sidewalk Café was that it's fairly quiet in the winter. Mike plays cool jazz on the sound system, and it's usually possible to talk.

Rollie was sitting at one of the front tables, holding a beer bottle in his hand. He rose when we came in. "Hi, Lee, Joe," he said. "Did you know that if Rosie O'Donnell married one of the Bush brothers — and decided to take a more formal name to suit her new status — she'd be Rose Bush?"

We groaned, then ditched our coats and ordered our own drinks. A glass of white wine for me, and scotch for Joe. The scotch request surprised me, since I know Joe hates the stuff. Then I realized he didn't really plan to drink it, since he was driving. The drink was simply stage dressing.

I left the talking to Joe.

"You know that Lee's been trying to understand what happened thirty-odd years ago, when her mom became Warner Pier's runaway bride."

"Yes, that was a seven-day wonder." Rollie nodded and smiled his usual smile, the one I didn't understand. "It caused more comment than that trip to Lansing."

Joe ignored the Lansing reference and spoke again. "We found out that you were a bearer at Bill Dykstra's funeral. So you must have known him pretty well. What did you think of him?"

Rollie chuckled. "I wasn't really buddies with Bill, of course. I'd taught him. His mom and I taught together."

"Why did they ask you to be a bearer?"

"I don't have any idea, but it's not a request you can refuse. As for Bill, well — I guess until that summer I'd thought he was an ordinary guy. Mr. Straight. Like his older brother the Eagle Scout, but then Ed went nuts — I guess you've heard about that?"

We both nodded, and Rollie went on. "Yeah, Ed infuriated his dad by going to Canada. It was Bill who stayed home and acted like Mr. Good Guy. Then he committed suicide. Who'da thunk it?"

"So Bill's suicide really surprised you?"

"At the time it did, Joe. Later, well, you remember things you didn't give any significance at the time."

"Such as?"

"Bill was getting desperate to get away from home. I see it now. I guess that's why . . ." His voice trailed off.

I spoke then. "I've gathered that both my mom and Bill were eager to get away from their families. I recognize that's probably a major reason they wanted to get married."

Rollie laughed again. "That was one reason. But thirty years ago things were different, Lee. Kids wanted to get married — how can I put this delicately? Because it was the only way to guarantee a regular . . ."

"Sex life?" I said.

I was pleased to see Rollie blush slightly. "Well, yes. Of course, we'd been through the sixties, and things were changing. But change hadn't hit Warner Pier yet. Some doctors were still refusing to prescribe the pill to unmarried girls, for example. We all thought Bill and Sally wanted to get married for the usual reasons, the reasons people had married young for centuries.

"But looking back — after Bill's suicide — I guess I did see more desperation in his outlook those past few months. That's purely hindsight."

We all sat quietly for a moment, then Joe leaned forward. "Rollie," he said, "Lee said you offered to tell her mom something important about Bill Dykstra. Can you share that information with us instead?"

Rollie frowned and sipped his drink. "I'm not sure I should. Didn't I hear that Sally's coming for a visit this week? Why don't I talk to her?"

"She's just making a quick trip. She may not be able to see you."

"I'm not sure, Joe. I know that Sally wouldn't want this to get out . . ."

"You don't trust us? Come on, Rollie. Lee's trying to *protect* her mom. I don't know what you knew about Bill Dykstra, but I definitely don't think Lee should arrange for you to talk to her mom before she knows just what you're going to tell her."

Take that, Rollie, I thought. Tell us or don't tell anybody. Joe had laid it on the line. But would Rollie buy?

For a minute I didn't think he would. Our drinks came then, for one thing, and Rollie asked for a dish of peanuts. And he didn't say a word while the waitress got them for us. Then Rollie ate a handful. And we still didn't know if he was going to talk to us at all.

Then he leaned over the table. When he spoke, his voice was low. "Did you two know there was a lot of drug dealing going on in Warner County that summer?"

Joe shook his head, but I spoke. "I knew. I read all the *Gazettes* and *Dorinda News* issues for that summer."

"You knew Ed had a record? He'd been arrested for possession?"

"Yes, I was also told that Bill was very angry with his brother for getting involved with the drug scene."

Rollie grimaced. "I'm afraid his opinion changed that summer, Lee."

"Why do you say that?"

"Because Bill needed money — and all of a sudden he had a lot. He sure didn't get it repairing television sets."

CHAPTER 15

Whatever I'd been expecting, this wasn't it.

"No way!" I said.

Joe gripped my knee. "Do you have any evidence, any facts to support that, Rollie?"

"I'm afraid not, Joe. But I knew Lovie pretty well in those days. I know she was worried about it."

Rollie smiled his usual smile, crinkling his eyes into mere slits. "It does seem out of character for Bill, doesn't it? But Bill and Sally were determined to move to Chicago. They were young and naïve. Bill told me they were shocked at how expensive renting an apartment was."

That rang true. I could remember my first attempt at moving out of my mom's place. I was nineteen, I'd found a roommate, and we looked at apartments near UT Dallas. My roommate said she'd get a student loan, but ol' Lee — with a phobia about debt instilled by her parents' hundreds of arguments over money — decided to stay with Mama another year. A year later, when I couldn't stand my mom's place any longer, I had to work full-time to support my housing and could only take half a college load each semester. I didn't get my accounting degree until I was twenty-seven and had been married and divorced.

Anyway, I understood the financial pressure of establishing a home, even on the cheap. But getting money through selling drugs would be a risky way to earn an apartment deposit, and — morals aside — everybody who had known Bill had agreed that he was practical. I didn't find Rollie's speculations believable.

I might have argued with Rollie, but Joe nudged me, looked at his watch, and said that we'd better leave. Joe paid the tab; then we headed for Holland. I don't think either of us said a word for the whole thirty miles. We were in a booth in the restaurant and had ordered dinner, raising our voices to be heard over the background noise, before we began to communicate again.

After the waitress left, Joe moved around to my side of the booth, bringing his silverware with him. I looked at him in some surprise. He wasn't usually that insistent on close proximity in public.

He put his lips close to my ear. "I don't want to yell about this," he said, "but what did you think of Rollie's idea?"

"The idea that Bill Dykstra sold drugs? I think it's stupid."

"I suppose it would be some sort of explanation, Lee. Bill might have been hauled in for questioning or something, made to see that the jig was up. So he decided to send your mom away to get her out of the mess, then committed suicide to get himself out of it. It could also explain your mom's concern about the sheriff. He would have been the one to investigate rural drug deals."

"But everybody agrees that Bill was very down-to-earth and practical, Joe. Selling drugs would be an awfully risky way to build up your savings account."

"I agree."

"It simply seems screwy to me."

"Maybe Hogan can find out something."

"And I can talk to Mom about it. After she gets here Saturday."

Joe stayed on my side of the booth, and after a moment of silence, I turned to face him. "Joe, I've got a question."

"Shoot."

"For months now Rollie has been twitting you about Lansing."

Joe gave a deep sigh. "I keep hoping he'll get over that."

"What is he talking about?"

"I guess Rollie's trying to threaten me. I probably should put the whole story in the *Gazette.* Tell the world, and then he'd get off my back."

"Forget it," I said. "I don't want to be part of Rollie's little game."

Joe laughed. "It's just something stupid that happened when I was in high school."

"We all did stupid things in high school."

"Yes, but this was unusually stupid. A bunch of us went to Lansing for a speech competition held during the state fair. We stayed at a motel. Rollie was one of the chaperones."

"Fat lot of good he'd be."

"Well, he was better than a couple of the moms who were along. They went off to visit friends and left the whole group on its own for an evening. Didn't get back until way after midnight." He sighed. "I won't go into all the details — they'd embarrass some otherwise innocent people — but we got some beer, held quite a party, and wound up skinny-dipping in the hotel pool around one a.m."

"Oh, gee! Did Rollie catch you?"

"Yep. He chased us all back to our rooms."

"And you were all in trouble."

"Nope. He didn't blab. But now and then, over the years, he's hinted that he might yet tell the story."

He turned and looked at me. "I figured out that he gets more fun out of threatening us than he would have seeing that we were properly disciplined at the time."

"That's ugly!"

"I agree. I guess that's why I've always been wary of Rollie. He likes to feel as if he's forcing people to do things."

We sat through a movie that I now have no recollection of seeing, and Joe was dropping me off at Aunt Nettie's when he caught his breath. "Oh! Is it Saturday your mom is flying in?"

"Yes. Three thirty."

"I need to haul a boat to Grand Rapids Saturday. If she wouldn't mind riding in the truck, we could pick her up."

"She's renting a car. I think it's stupid — we've got my van and Aunt Nettie's Buick, and neither of us minds sharing. But she insisted."

"If you wanted to meet her, I could drop you at the airport. You could ride down to Warner Pier with her."

I laughed. "I could surprise her. She might not like it, but we could talk on the way down here."

We agreed that this was a good idea. One thirty was named as our departure time, since Grand Rapids is a little over an hour away.

On Friday morning I went by the police station and made a statement about finding Sheriff Van Hoosier's body. After Hogan quizzed me, I quizzed him, trying to get an idea of how the investigation into Van Hoosier's death was going. Hogan wasn't directly involved, supposedly, but he'd obviously been talking to the Michigan State Police and the Warner County sheriff about the crime.

He didn't tell me anything in plain English, but his questions focused on what time Joe and I had arrived at the Pleasant Creek Senior apartments. He also asked if we'd seen anybody come in the back door.

"Back door? I didn't even notice a back door, Hogan."

"They've got to have one, Lee. To use as a fire door, if nothing else."

"That makes sense. I suppose it's at the end of the hall, which would be right next door to Van Hoosier's room. But it must have been closed. I didn't notice a draft, anyway."

"I guess the residents aren't supposed to

go out that door, and the visitors aren't supposed to come in by it. But probably people who live down at that end let their visitors in and out that way."

"If you parked at that end of the building, it would be a lot shorter than walking clear back to the central desk," I said. "But I didn't notice anything about it. Maybe Joe did."

"He says not."

That ended my session with Hogan. I called the shop to make sure nothing major was going on. Nothing was. So I went to the library to look at microfilm, finishing up my project to read all the papers from the summer my mother ran away from home. I'd brought a sandwich from home, so I could eat lunch at my desk to make up part of the time.

I tried to go over the twelve *Gazette* issues from that summer carefully, not reading every story, of course, but checking out every headline for connections with crime. I did come up with one thing that was interesting.

"Break-in Reported At Closed Cottage"

The crime itself wasn't too unusual, of course. Summer cottages, to this day, are apparently considered fair game by local juvenile delinquents and other lawbreakers.

It's easy to spot an unoccupied summer cottage because the windows are normally covered with shutters. And those shutters are designed to protect the cottages from the winter elements, not from burglars. They aren't usually the type of shutters that are attached to the window frame with hinges. They're separate slabs, usually of several boards nailed together on crosspieces, something like the side of a packing crate.

Shutters are taken down when the cottage is opened for the summer. Yet this cottage was described as "closed," which on the east coast of Lake Michigan means the shutters were still up. In fact, the person making the report said entry had been made by "removing a shutter." Which would be like trying to handle Huck Finn's raft if it was standing on one end and had been nailed to a wall.

That was slightly surprising, but the two main shockers in the brief story were yet to come.

First, the cottage had belonged to Benson McKay III, of Chicago. And second, the person making the report was Ed Dykstra, caretaker.

Bill Dykstra's father had been caretaker for the McKay family cottage.

What a coincidence.

I drove back to the office and tried to work, but that coincidence kept popping into my mind.

Sheriff Van Hoosier, according to his nurse, had mentioned my mother's name in connection to a kidnapping.

Quinn McKay had been kidnapped the summer my mom ran away from her hometown, refusing ever to return.

My mom's fiancé had been the son of the caretaker for the McKay summer cottage.

So? So what?

Quinn had been kidnapped in Chicago. And he escaped or was released by the kidnappers in southern Illinois. The crime had occurred hundreds of miles from Warner Pier.

It was all a coincidence. It had to be.

Unless Bill Dykstra had been involved in the kidnapping somehow.

I slammed a desk drawer. That was a truly stupid idea. Everyone described Bill as absolutely on the up-and-up. Everybody but Rollie. How could I think Bill could be involved in a kidnapping?

I resolved to put the whole matter out of my mind until I could talk to my mom. But the whole matter didn't want to stay out of my mind. I didn't accomplish much that afternoon.

The evening was a little better. I spent it clearing out Aunt Nettie's extra bedroom, stacking all my wedding paraphernalia in boxes and piles in my own room, taking extra clothes from that room's closet and hanging them in my own closet.

One of the things I moved was my wedding dress. I'd bought it at a high-toned shop in Grand Rapids, and it hadn't been cheap. After I moved it, I yielded to temptation and tried it on again.

The dress wasn't a poufy white thing. In line with our plan to have a small, simple wedding, I'd picked out a dress in champagne, a color with too much orange in it to be called beige. It was basically a shirtdress with a lace bodice. It had no collar, a slightly dropped waistline, long sleeves, and a row of tiny covered buttons down the front. The knee-length skirt was a floaty chiffon. I hadn't ordered my shoes yet, but I wanted them dyed to match, with small heels. Joe is several inches taller than I am, but four-inch heels would be pushing it.

Joe hadn't seen the dress, but I thought he'd like it. The color was going to make my hazel eyes look brownish or greenish and would look great with the bouquet of yellow roses he had asked that I carry. All Texas girls get yellow roses sometime in their lives.

I hated to take the dress off, but I did. I hung it carefully on its padded hanger and draped a plastic cover over it, ready to show it to my mom. I'd sent her a picture earlier.

Aunt Nettie brought up clean sheets, and we made the bed.

"Mom will be surprised by the room," I said. "You've fixed it up really nicely."

"You don't think Sally will be disappointed because it's not like her childhood room?"

"To be honest, Aunt Nettie, I think she'll be pleased."

Yes, my mom had apparently wanted to forget her childhood and youth. She wouldn't want her room to be the same.

I went into the office for a couple of hours Saturday morning. Between the wedding and my researches into what happened thirty-three years earlier, I was way behind on my work. One of our high school helpers, Tracy, was working the counter. Dolly Jolly was in charge of a Saturday chocolate-making crew, and they were busy. I had eaten the lunch I'd brought along and was ready to go when I saw Joe's pickup outside, pulling a boat trailer.

This particular boat, he reminded me, was

one we had picked up from its owner the previous summer. It belonged to an executive of a Grand Rapids office furniture company. A bad guy had followed us as we drove it back to Warner Pier and had tried to run us into a bridge abutment. Only Joe's skillful driving and experience at hauling boats had averted disaster.

"I wish you hadn't reminded me of that episode," I said. "Have you been working on the boat since clear last summer?"

"Off and on. You know, you put on a coat of lacquer, then let it cure for a couple of months." Joe grinned. "What's the use of being your own boss, if you don't push your customers around? Anyway, the boat can't go in the water until May or June."

"I guess the owner wants to put the boat in the garage and gloat over it."

"It did turn out nice." Joe sounded complacent. I laughed and told him so.

"Why shouldn't I sound complacent? I'm finally making some money by fooling around with boats. I've figured out a way to justify keeping my law license without being tied down to an office and to clients I think are jerks." He reached over and caressed my knee. "And I'm about to marry the smartest girl in Michigan. And she's not bad looking, either."

"As long as you've got your priorities straight."

We had a pleasant drive for two-thirds of the way; then traffic came to a dead halt. A truck was jackknifed on the interstate, and it had apparently hit another car. We could see flashing lights ahead. All sorts of emergency vehicles and personnel were working like mad. We sat in the truck, completely stalled, for an hour.

It was getting later and later.

Getting off the interstate wasn't an option, because we were nowhere near an exit. We simply had to sit there. I began to check my watch. Then Joe began to check his. We sat. I turned the radio on. After ten minutes I turned it off. Joe turned the motor off. The truck's cab got cold. He started the motor again and warmed the cab up. He turned the motor off.

Finally I began to laugh. "It's going to be ridiculous if I ride up to Grand Rapids with you and miss my mom and simply have to hitch a ride back in the truck."

"As long as you see the ridiculous side of it. Does your mom have a cell phone?"

"I'm sure she does, but she just uses it for work. She's never given me the number."

My mom's plane was due in thirty minutes when we began to move again, and it was arrival time for the flight before we got to Gerald Ford Airport. Joe offered to park and come in with me. "We need to make sure you haven't missed her," he said.

I shook my head. "You've got your cell, don't you?"

Joe nodded.

"Just let me out. If I need a ride back to Warner Pier, I'll call you."

I dashed into the terminal and skidded to a stop in front of one of those overhead monitors that give clues about when and where planes are to arrive. Mom's flight was already on the ground, and it had arrived at B concourse.

The Grand Rapids airport is the size I like for an airport, big enough to be served by six or eight airlines, but small enough that you can get around it easily. There are only two concourses, and both feed into a large central waiting area, surrounded with the traditional restaurants, gift shops, playrooms for kids, and workrooms for business travelers. But there are two ways out of that central waiting area. I decided it might be smarter to wait for my mom at the rental car desk. She could be going down one passage while I was going up the other one.

Of course, I didn't know which car rental agency she was going to, but there were only four, and the desks were all close together. So I lurked between Avis and Thrifty, trying to convince myself that Mom was going to be glad to see me.

People were going by in a steady stream, though the Grand Rapids airport is nothing like DFW or O'Hare. I wasn't far from the luggage carousels. But I kept a sharp eye on the closest passage, a wide ramp leading down from that central waiting area.

When I saw my mom come down the passage, I was surprised to see that she was smiling broadly and talking to a man in a heavy overcoat. He was wearing a warm hat, the dress-up kind. It might even have been made from some sort of fur, and he had pulled it down over his forehead. All I could see of his face was a big nose. He was pulling a small bag — definitely the carry-on type. Mom was carrying her coat over her arm, and clutching the big tote bag she used as a purse when traveling.

I wondered who the guy was. Mom hadn't mentioned knowing anybody in Grand Rapids, and I didn't think she would have taken up with a seatmate. But you never can tell. I stepped back a bit, waiting to see which rental desk she approached.

Mom stopped and swung her coat around, and her companion set the wheeled suitcase on its end. He took her coat and helped her into it gallantly. Mom buttoned up, took a scarf from her pocket, and wrapped it around her neck.

Then the man in the dark coat and furry hat grabbed the suitcase's handle again and gestured toward the door. Mom didn't even glance toward the car rental desks. She nodded and preceded the man out the door of the terminal.

CHAPTER 16

My mom was leaving the airport with some strange man.

I was so surprised that it took me a moment to start running after her. I had to weave through a large family party and almost knocked two business-types flat before I got to the automatic doors that opened to the outside. I stopped on the sidewalk and looked both ways. I didn't want her to get away from me. For one thing, I needed a ride.

There she was. Mom and her well-dressed escort were nearly across the pedestrian walkway that led to the parking lot.

"Mom!" I yelled, but she didn't turn around. I went after her, trying to place my feet carefully and still cover the ground quickly. The walkway had been cleared of snow, but vehicles ran over it all day long, dropping bits of ice, snow, and slush to form an obstacle course.

Ahead I saw the back of my mom's well-kept blond head, and the dressy black coat that disguised her erect, pouter-pigeon figure — slightly swaybacked and with a big bosom. I could see the well-dressed man better now, too. He was looking down at her, and I caught his profile. He had an enormous nose, and somehow he seemed familiar. Was he someone from Warner Pier? I couldn't think who.

"Mom!" I yelled again, but my mom's head didn't turn. I guess she wasn't expecting to be hailed as "Mom" in the Grand Rapids airport.

"Sally! Sally McKinney!" I yelled the words as loudly as I could, and I finally got a reaction.

Mom whirled around. "Lee!" She smiled and moved toward me. Her escort caught at her arm, and Mom pulled away. For a moment I thought he wasn't going to let go. "It's my daughter," Mom said. She yanked her arm from his grasp.

By then I had caught up with her, and we were hugging each other.

After a few *It's so good to see you*s and *You look great*s, Mom grinned at me. "I didn't expect to be met in person, not after the elegant welcome you arranged."

"Welcome?"

"The limo ride."

"Huh?" I could feel my jaw drop, and my mom gestured behind her. "The upgrade to a larger car. The escort at the gate and limo to the rental lot. That's what I call elegant."

"Sorry. If you got special treatment, I'm afraid it wasn't because of anything I did."

"But the escort said . . ." Mom sounded puzzled, and she looked around, apparently ready to question the well-dressed gent.

But he wasn't there. While my mom and I had been greeting each other, he had disappeared. All that was left was Mom's small pull-along suitcase, abandoned in the middle of the parking lot.

I gawked all around, for once blessing my height, and I saw a furry hat moving rapidly away from us. The well-dressed man was already two rows away and heading to the left at the rate of a speed skater.

"I don't understand," Mom said. "He met me with a sign and was real friendly."

"A sign?"

"Yes. 'Sally McKinney.' He held up a card with my name."

Someone had met my mother at the gate with a sign? He had told her he was to escort her to an upgraded rental vehicle? Then he ran away when I showed up? Why? Why would all this happen?

The answer kicked me in the pit of the stomach. Someone had tried to kidnap my mother.

"Mom! Go back to the terminal! Find the security guard. I'll try to get his license number!"

"License number?" Mom sounded completely confused.

"Go back to the terminal!"

The airport parking lot funnels all exiting traffic to one end of the lot. I cut though the parked cars, bearing toward that end. Maybe I could get a look at the car the big-nosed, well-dressed man had been driving. Maybe I could get a look at him. Maybe I'd even recognize him. Maybe I could even stop him, though that might not be a bright idea.

The parking lot, thank heavens, wasn't crowded, and it had been plowed. I lost sight of the fur-hatted gent, but I heard a car door slam in the direction he'd been running. Then a motor roared, and I saw a big black car move out of its parking place on the next row over.

I dashed between a van and a pickup, trying to get into the lane of traffic that Fur Hat would be leaving by. If I could just get a good look at him and get his license number . . .

I might have, too, if I hadn't skidded on a chunk of ice. I realized I was about to go flying out into the traffic lane, right in front of the big black car. Somehow I didn't feel confident about the car stopping.

As I started to fall, I desperately grabbed at the grille of the pickup. This pulled a muscle in my shoulder, but it kept me from falling headlong in front of the black car. I saw the furry hat though the windshield; then I pivoted and sat down on the pickup's front bumper. A long black Lincoln roared by, but I couldn't see anything through the heavily tinted side windows. I jumped up, still hanging onto the grille, but I stepped on another chunk of ice and realized I was going down again. I had time for just a glimpse of the black car's tag. It wasn't a Michigan tag, and it was leaving the area rapidly.

I regained a fairly firm footing and stood there in the slushy parking lot, staring at the departing car. By then the Lincoln had turned into another lane and was almost out of sight. I started trying to brush the mud from the pickup's bumper off my jeans and ski jacket.

"Lee! Lee! Are you all right?"

Mom was picking her way across the parking lot. She wore boots, but they were indoor, high-heeled boots designed for a Dallas business office. Suddenly I was terribly annoyed with her.

"I told you to go back to the terminal," I said angrily.

"Are you all right?"

"I may have pulled a muscle, but I'll live. Which is more than you might."

"What do you mean?"

"Do you think that guy was kidnapping you so he could take you out to dinner?"

"Kidnapping me?" Mom rolled her eyes. "Honestly, Lee. You live such a dramatic life."

That set the tone for the next half hour of our relationship.

My mom thought I was imagining the trouble she'd barely avoided, and I thought she was deliberately misunderstanding the situation. I didn't help matters by getting my tongue tied in knots after I rushed up to an airport security officer and blurted out the whole story.

"Just a mix-up," Mom told the guard, a burly blond guy with a crew cut.

"Missile, my left foot," I said. "I mean mix-up! It was no mix-up. It was a delicate kidney attester. I mean, kidnapping attempt." I made myself slow down. "It was a deliberate kidnapping attempt. And it was dumb lust — I mean, luck! It was only dumb luck that kept it from being successful."

The burly blond guy grinned, and I ground my teeth. The Grand Rapids Police, of course, had officers on duty at the airport, and one of them joined us. That guy — even taller and burlier than the security man — didn't look convinced either. I tried to reach Hogan Jones on my cell phone, to ask him to tell the Grand Rapids authorities that I wasn't a complete idiot. But Hogan wasn't available, and the name of a village police chief — one with a force of five if you counted the dispatcher — didn't impress either officer. Hogan knows people on the Grand Rapids force, but apparently neither of these guys had met him.

"I'm sure it was just a mix-up," Mom repeated. "The escort must have been sent to pick up some other passenger. Then, when Lee ran up to us, he saw that he had the wrong person. He was embarrassed and went away." The blond guy nodded his crew cut, and the Grand Rapids cop looked stony.

I tried to stick to my guns: "But you said he carried a sign with your name on it, Mom. Sally McKinney."

"Maybe I was mistaken, Lee. Maybe it was just 'McKinney.' Or it could have been some other 'Mc' name. McKennon, maybe. Or McSomething else."

"The man wasn't carrying a sign when I saw you," I said. "What happened to it?"

Mom looked puzzled. "I don't really remember. Could he have simply dropped it into the trash?"

"We can look," I said. I stalked back toward the gate, leading a procession of the crew cut security man, a uniformed Grand Rapids cop, and my mom, who was still objecting to the whole process with every step. We retraced my mom's steps, going back to the passageway that she would have come down after disembarking, and having her identify the spot where her well-dressed escort had been waiting. We looked in the nearest trash container. It held no sign, and no pieces of cardboard that could have once been a sign.

I led them on through the big waiting room. She'd made a stop at the ladies room, Mom said, and the escort had stood outside. There was a trash container at that spot. No sign was in it.

To my relief, Joe showed up then. I'd called his cell phone before we'd even reached the security office, but he had taken time to deliver the boat before he came back to the airport.

Of course, he had to hear the whole story from the beginning. And once more Mom assured everyone the whole thing was some sort of mix-up.

I was steaming, which meant I was talking more like an idiot than ever. "I know that my mom had a narrow estate. I mean, escape! That man tried to thatch her. I mean, snatch her!"

"But there's no physical evidence," the security guard said, "and your mom thinks it was just a mistake."

I looked for Joe, but he'd disappeared. So had the Grand Rapids cop.

"I appreciate your concern for your mother," the security man said, "but there's no physical evidence."

"And what physical evidence could there be?"

"How about this?" It was Joe's voice.

We all swung toward it, and I saw that he was coming out of the men's room. Using a paper towel, he was holding a handful of torn cardboard. He showed us the top piece. "cKi" it read. We all crowded into the business center and laid the pieces out on a worktable, assembling them like a jigsaw puzzle.

The pieces spelled out "Sally McKinney."

"See," I said to my mom. "He *was* trying

to snatch you."

But my mom's jaw was clamped into that firm, Dutch line that I'd learned meant she and I were about to have a fight.

"It doesn't prove anything," she said. "All it proves is that he thought — thought — he was supposed to meet me. He had the wrong person, that's all. He must have looked at the wrong list. If we ask at the Avis desk — which we should have done before imposing on the time of the security guards, I'm sure that they'll tell us he was supposed to meet someone else on that flight."

She took a deep and determined breath, then went on. "But at any rate, I'm sure it was only a mix-up, and I want to drop the matter."

The Grand Rapids policeman, who had been completely silent during the whole episode, finally spoke. "Would you be willing to sign a complaint?"

"No!" Mom's voice was extremely firm.

I took a breath as deep as my mom's had been and opened my mouth, ready to join battle.

But Joe surprised me by putting his arm around my shoulder. "Let it go, Lee," he said softly. "There's no point. We'll sort this out after we get home."

"But Mom doesn't know all the crazy things that have been happening around here," I said.

"What crazy things?" the Grand Rapids cop said.

"Oh, like strange —" The look on Mom's face stopped me cold. I realized that she didn't want me to bring up her history as a runaway bride, and it really didn't seem to be a good idea.

"What crazy things?" the cop repeated.

"Oh, my fiancé and I found a dead man two days ago."

Joe spoke quickly. "He was a patient in a nursing home."

The cop shrugged and appeared to have lost interest.

"Let's pick up your mom's car and get on home," Joe said again.

I began to see that I might be better off keeping my mouth shut. If we could just get to Warner Pier, Hogan could advise me.

So the whole kidnapping episode ended in anticlimax. I tried again to talk Mom out of renting a car, assuring her that Joe's pickup was a perfectly comfortable vehicle for the ride to Warner Pier and that she could borrow my van the rest of her stay. But she wouldn't be convinced. A half hour later — by now it was getting dark — we were leaving Gerald Ford Airport in a mid-sized Chevy. Joe was following us. Mom put my name on the rental agreement, and she asked me to drive, since I knew the way. A new bypass had opened, making the trip to Warner Pier much shorter than it had been when she came to Michigan for Uncle Phil's funeral.

We didn't say much until we merged onto I-96. Then Mom turned to me and made that sound I always called a "significant sigh." When I was growing up, it usually meant I'd said or done the wrong thing and was going to hear about it.

But this time, she surprised me with praise.

"Lee, I did appreciate your efforts back there. And I'm sure you were right. That man did try to kidnap me."

"Mom! If you agreed that I was right, how could you refuse to sign a complaint!"

"Joe and that cop found the sign, and I noticed it was saved, in case I change my mind, and we need it as evidence someday. But you were not only right about the kidnapping attempt, you were right about something else. 'Strange things,' you said. A lot of strange things have been happening. And maybe we need to talk about them before we involve yet another law enforce-

240

ment agency."

She sighed again. "So I'm going to break down and tell you about the most embarrassing thing that ever happened to me. Or ever will happen to me."

Chocolate Chat:
1930s Chocolate

My grandmother Nettie Bohreer Waite saw her family through the Great Depression by managing a bakery in Ardmore, Oklahoma. Here's one of her chocolate cake recipes.

Gran's Fudge Cake with Mocha Frosting

2 1/2 cups sugar
2 sticks margarine
5 eggs, separated
1 teaspoon vanilla
1/4 cup cocoa
3 cups cake flour
1 teaspoon baking soda
1/2 teaspoon salt
1 cup buttermilk

Cream sugar and maragarine. Beat in egg yolks. Add vanilla. Add cocoa. Sift flour with soda and salt. Add to first mixture alternately with buttermilk. Beat egg whites stiff and fold in.

This makes four layers or one large sheet cake. Bake layers twenty to twenty-five minutes at 375 degrees or a sheet cake thirty-five to forty-five minutes at 350 degrees.

Mocha Frosting

1 stick margarine
4 tablespoons coffee
2 tablespoons cocoa
1 egg yolk
1 pound powdered sugar
Soften margarine, then mix all ingredients. Beat until smooth.

— *JoAnna Carl*

Chapter 17

My head whipped toward Mom. I swerved slightly and nearly hit a passing car, but I got back into my own lane before his horn stopped blaring.

Embarrassing? Mom was going to tell me about her most embarrassing moment? People don't leave their homes because they're embarrassed. What could this have to do with all the suspicious things that had happened?

Mom was giving another deep sigh. "You probably wouldn't even think it was embarrassing," she said. "Your generation, I mean. Times have changed so much. But Bill and I — I know the sexual revolution had happened before our engagement, but it hadn't hit Warner Pier High. Oh, we all knew that Ed — Bill's brother — had lived in a commune, and there were whispers about what went on there. But the kids in high school still talked about who was 'doing it.' And my mother — Oh, Lee, sometimes I'm glad you never knew my mother."

"Aunt Nettie said she had sort of come unglued after your dad died."

"That's the politest way it can be expressed. Yelling, screaming, crying. I don't think that Phil and Nettie knew what was going on at all."

"Aunt Nettie says they didn't. She says they were so focused on starting their business . . . I think she feels that they let you down."

"I never blamed them because our mom was nuts. But one of the things she was nuts about was making sure that Bill and I didn't have sex. She would question me. Where did we go? What did we do? She didn't come out and say what she was afraid of — she seemed to be afraid of the word — but her meaning was clear."

Mom laughed, though the sound wasn't humorous. "She was trying so hard to keep us celibate and was so sure that we were going to rip our clothes off and go at it if we got a chance that she had the opposite-opposite effect, if you can understand what I mean. I became self-conscious, scared of having sex. On the day of the rehearsal, if she'd asked me if I wanted to call the wedding off, I'm afraid I would have."

"Maybe that's why you were willing to leave when Bill told you to."

"No, the evening of the rehearsal things took quite a different path." Mom sighed again. "Vita and Ed Dykstra had everybody over for a picnic dinner after the rehearsal. It was really nice. Vita was a wonderful cook. And she was so creative. You probably know that."

I realized that I'd never told Mom that Vita Dykstra had changed into Lovie, the town nut, running around collecting aluminum cans. I decided this wasn't the moment, and Mom went on.

"Anyway, it was a lovely evening, and everyone was being so nice — including Bill. He really was a sweetheart, and I was realizing how lucky I was to get him. It was all fine until we were leaving, and Mother blew it. The minister was shaking my hand and making the kind of glowing remarks the occasion called for — about young love and a happy future — and Mother pops up and says, 'Yes, Reverend Vanoss. Now I won't have to worry about her getting pregnant.' "

"That wasn't cool!"

"No! I was so crushed I began to cry. I said, 'You've never had to worry about that!' And I ran off and got in Bill's car. I think maybe Mother started to come after me, but Bill stopped her. I could see him talking to her. Bill was always tactful, you know. I'm sure he told her he'd calm me down and bring me home. Of course, that made me madder than ever. I felt that he was taking her side. When Bill got in the car, he must have thought he was sharing the front seat with a buzz saw."

"Poor guy."

"Oh, he handled it. He took my hand, and he said, 'Tomorrow night we'll be on our honeymoon.' And he kissed my palm."

"And he was how old? Twenty? He really was a peach, Mom."

"Yes, like I said, Bill was always calming people down. He'd had plenty of chances to perfect that trait in the last couple of years, with his brother and his dad being at odds, and his mom caught in the middle. A bad situation."

"I heard a few things about that."

"Anyway, Bill and I left the party. We went out to our regular parking place, which was behind the big shed at the McKay cottage."

"Bill's father was the caretaker, right?"

"You knew that?"

"I found out accidentally."

"The cottage hadn't been opened that summer, so the property was secluded and

. . . well, we parked there."

"Naturally, Mom."

"I said your generation wouldn't be embarrassed by what happened. But, remember, I was still a virgin. Here it was the night before our wedding, and we'd never actually 'done it,' as the kids said. But a couple of things had changed. First, I'd gone to the doctor the month before, and I was now on the pill."

Mother turned toward me. "I went without consulting my mother. Would you believe it? She didn't think a young girl needed to have a pelvic exam before she got married. And she knew Bill and I didn't want to have kids right away, but she wouldn't even discuss birth control with me. Or sex, for that matter. I got a book from the library."

"You did much better with me, Mom."

"If I did, it was in spite of her, not because of any lesson I learned from her."

"You said two things had changed. What was the second one?"

Mom thought about it a moment. "I guess the second one was Mother's unfortunate remark."

"That she didn't need to worry about your getting pregnant?"

"Yes. I finally rebelled."

248

"A lot of kids would have rebelled a lot earlier."

"Bill had always gone along with my decision, bless him, but he was just a regular twenty-year-old guy. When it became clear that I'd changed my mind from 'slow down' to 'go ahead,' he reached in his pocket and came out with a key. 'Let's not stay here, in the car,' he said. 'Let's go someplace special.' I said I'd be afraid to go to a motel, but he grinned real big and said that wasn't it.

"Bill got a flashlight out of the glove box, and a blanket out of the trunk. Then he led me onto the back porch of the McKay house. The key he had was to the back door. He'd snitched it from his dad.

"I was nervous — fearful, but excited. I said, 'What if some of the McKays come?' But Bill said the father and stepmother were in Europe, and that Quinn was in Chicago.

"The electricity was off, but Bill used his flashlight to show me the kitchen, which was small, and the living room, which was nice, but not elegant. Antique-y. Then he said, 'This is what I wanted you to see,' and he took me into a bedroom that was right off the living room. And it *was* elegant, but with a rustic twist. Stone fireplace. Four-poster bed carved to look like tree trunks. Heck, those posts looked like *redwood* trunks, real heavy."

"It doesn't really sound like a lakeshore cottage ought to look, Mom."

"Thinking back, I'd say it was in the worst possible taste. But Mr. McKay — he was always bringing home a new wife, and that's what the current one had wanted, I guess. I remember that the windows had heavy drapes with elaborate wooden cornices." She laughed. "It was really something, a sort of a Victorian brothel. Anyway, it didn't take long for Bill to spread his blanket on the bed — we weren't so passionate that we forgot that we didn't want to leave a mess — not even dirty sheets. And — well, we took our clothes off and got on that fancy bed."

She quit talking, and I didn't say anything either.

"We got pretty involved with each other, but before anything had actually — well, happened! — this blinding light began flashing around the living room."

She turned toward me and put her hands to her head in a frantic gesture. "Lee, if I live to be a hundred, nothing will ever scare me like that did."

I didn't know if I should laugh or cry. The thought of the innocent almost-bride and groom — ages eighteen and twenty — getting caught in a fantasy bedroom in a lonely cottage was right out of a sex comedy. But what might have been funny in the movies would not have been the least bit humorous in real life.

"How awful!" I said. "So you weren't as alone as you thought. What did you do?"

"I slid off the bed on the opposite side from the door. Then I crawled around to the foot, trying to find my clothes while not making a single sound. Of course, Bill was doing the same thing on the other side of the bed. We might have been able to hide — get into the closet or something — except that Bill stepped on my hand, and I yelped. Oh, it was a scene from a smutty comedy. A nightmare.

"Somebody out in the living room said, 'What's that?' and came to the door and flashed the light around the bedroom. Bill and I were spotlighted — both of us still stark naked.

"I was sure, of course, that it was Bill's dad. After all, he was caretaker for the place, and they'd had some problem with prowlers, so I thought he'd come around to check. So I was embarrassed, but not frightened. Then the person laughed! Laughed!

"Bill said, 'Ed?' I thought he was talking

to his dad. At first I couldn't figure out why he was calling his dad by his first name."

I gasped. "Ed? Was it Bill's brother? The one who had gone to Canada?"

"At the time, I couldn't figure out who it was. Bill told me to get dressed, and he grabbed his clothes and took them out into the living room. He left the flashlight, but he closed the door behind him. And I began to try to scramble into my clothes."

"I'd have been shaking too hard to button a button."

"I was wearing some sort of a granny dress, I think. I managed to get it on backward, I remember, and had to take it off and try again. And one of my sandals was under the bed. I had to get under there with the spiderwebs to find it. I finally managed to get everything on, and then I sat down at this weird dressing table — carved weirdly, I mean. I swear it had gargoyles on the legs. I sat there and cried."

"You were just a kid!"

"I was really too young to be getting married, though I did love Bill. But right at that moment I was so embarrassed and terrified I could have died. And the noises coming from the living room didn't help."

"What was happening?"

"Let's call it raised voices."

"Bill and Ed were arguing?"

"Bill and Ed and someone else. There was another voice. They were all talking at once. This strange voice yelled. 'Just go outside!' The voice sounded kind of familiar, but I never have been able to figure out who it was. Once Ed yelled, 'Shut up, Ratso!' I remember that — because of that movie with Dustin Hoffman. Then I heard Bill yell. He said, 'You'll go to jail, and they'll throw away the key!' I remember that. And Ed — I guess it was Ed — yelled back. 'I guess you want to turn Lake Michigan into a sewer!' "

"That was an odd thing to say, in the circumstances."

"Not if you knew Ed. He was absolutely fanatic on stopping pollution. Definitely a Greenpeace type. Militant. He turned every argument into something about the environment — no matter what the topic started out as."

"What finally happened?"

"I sat there, scared and crying, and I decided that I had to get out of there, one way or another. And I didn't want to go out through the living room, where the argument was going on. So I began to explore around the bedroom. Looked at all the windows and such."

253

"Since the shutters were up, that wouldn't have been a very easy way to get out."

"Actually, there was an outside door. Of course, I'd known it was there, because Bill and I had hung around the house a lot that summer. I should have thought of it immediately. It led to a deck outside the master bedroom. And the deck was an extension of the porch that went all around the house."

"The door wasn't shuttered?"

"No. It was a heavy, solid door with a deadbolt, and it wasn't shuttered like the windows were. Of course, right at that moment all I wanted to do was disappear. That door looked like the door to heaven."

"It didn't have a key lock?"

"Yes, it did. I was still exploring around with the flashlight, and I found the key to the house where Bill had left it on the bedside table. And it worked the deadbolt lock. In fact, I think the lock had just been lubricated, and it opened very easily — didn't make a sound. So I opened it and ran outside — and that's when I had the worst shock of the whole ghastly evening."

"What else could happen, Mom! A dinosaur or something?"

"Worse. I slipped out, flashing my light around, and that light hit the face of a strange man!"

I gasped, but I must have rolled my eyes at the same time. This whole tale was worthy of the plot of some sort of romance novel. Absolutely crazy. I would have thought Mom made the whole thing up, except that she'd never displayed that sort of imagination before.

"A strange man?" I'm afraid my voice showed my skepticism.

"Actually, after a moment I realized that I knew who it was. But it was still an awful shock."

"Who was it?"

"It was Quinn McKay."

"What was he doing there?"

"I didn't stop to ask. I screamed the house down."

"I can imagine."

"Bill began to yell. 'If you guys have done anything to hurt Sally, I'll kill you!' And other stuff like that. He was coming around the back of the house, and I ran that way. We whammed together on the side porch, and I screamed again. Bill grabbed my hand, and we ran for the shed and Bill's car. We jumped in. Ed had followed us. He came up to Bill's window and was beating on it. His hair was flying, and he had a lot of hair. He looked like a madman. Bill started the motor, and we dug out of there."

Mom gave a sort of sob. "Bill told me to make sure no one was following us — we were going through some sort of a back road that really needed a Jeep, and we didn't have one. But nobody came after us. So Bill drove me home."

"When did he send you to Chicago?"

"As soon as we got to my house. We sat in the drive a minute, and he asked if I could get my clothes out of the house without waking my mom up. I said that was easy — she'd been taking sleeping pills. But I didn't understand why he wanted me to. That's when Bill said he had to go back to the McKay cottage and 'take care of things.' "

"What things?"

"I couldn't get him to explain. But he was absolutely insistent that I leave. Right that minute. I was to go to Chicago, but I wasn't to go to the apartment we'd rented. I was to go to the hotel where we'd stayed on our senior trip and wait until he contacted me. He gave me all the money he had on him. It was three hundred dollars."

"Not much to run away from home on."

"It was nearly thirty-five years ago, Lee. Money went farther. And Bill assured me he'd be in contact with me within twenty-four hours. Then he took me to South

Haven and left me at the all-night gas station out on the interstate. He told me to take a cab to the bookstore — that's where the bus stop was — at six a.m. The bus would come through before seven."

"So you did what Bill said."

"Right. I got to Chicago by noon, and I went to that hotel and checked in. Then I waited for Bill to call."

"But he didn't."

"No. I sat there all day, afraid to even go out and buy food or a magazine. I kept remembering he'd promised to call me within twenty-four hours. But twenty-four hours went by without a call. Forty-eight hours went by."

"What did you do?"

"Finally I decided I simply had to call him. So I got a lot of coins, and I went to a pay phone, and I called the Dykstras' house. Mrs. Dykstra answered. I could tell something was wrong as soon as I heard her voice."

"Did she tell you Bill had committed suicide?"

"She didn't use that word. I've always remembered that. She told me he was found dead on a back road — it was nowhere near the McKay house — and that the sheriff was investigating. I was shocked, but I told her Bill had sent me away and that I was sure he hadn't committed suicide."

"What did she say to that?"

"She said for me not to come back. She asked if I had enough money to stay a few days. When I said yes, she said for me not to tell her where I was, but to call her at the end of the week. If things hadn't been settled, she said, she'd send me more money."

"That is so strange! You should have been asked about what happened between Bill and his brother."

"I know. Even then, young and dumb as I was, I knew I needed to tell the law enforcement officials what had happened."

Mom took a deep breath. "So, the next day I called the sheriff."

"What! You called Van Hoosier?"

"Yes. I just felt that I had to."

"Did you tell him the whole story?"

"I left out the part about being naked. But I told him all the important stuff. About Ed being there. About seeing Quinn McKay."

"You were an important witness. Why didn't Van Hoosier come to pick you up?"

"I have no idea, Lee. I've never had any idea."

"What did he say?"

"He told me that Bill had given me exactly

258

the right advice. He said I should stay away. He told me to move to a different hotel and not tell anyone where I was."

"That's crazy!"

Mom wiped her eyes, crying openly now. "Lee, he told me never to come back to Warner Pier under any circumstances, or I could wind up either dead or in jail!"

CHAPTER 18

I was so outraged I couldn't speak. I took ten deep breaths before I could get a word out. And when I did speak I was completely incoherent.

"If somebody hadn't killed that creep before I met him," I said, "I might have done it myself. To run an innocuous — I mean an innocent! — an innocent girl out of town like that. It was, it was . . ." My vocabulary failed me, but I finally went on. "It was *immortal!* I mean, immoral!"

Mom began to laugh. She was still crying, of course, but my goofs had broken the tension, I guess. Anyway, she laughed for about a mile, taking a Kleenex from her purse and wiping her eyes.

I sighed. "I guess I'm glad you can laugh about it now, Mom. But you must have been absolutely terrified at the time. A young girl. Alone in a big city. You must have been running out of money by then."

"I admit I was getting close to the end of my resources. I'd bought a return bus ticket, however, and I told Sheriff Van Hoosier that. I said I couldn't stay away much longer. I told him I'd have to use that return bus ticket and come home because I was nearly out of money."

"Did that change his mind?"

"It seemed to make him think. He asked me where I was in Chicago. Then he said, 'No, don't tell me. Can you find the main Chicago post office?' I told him I'd manage that. And he said he'd send me a letter in care of general delivery. He promised to get it off that day and to send it special delivery, so I should have it the next day. Then he said something really odd. He said, 'Sister, is there someplace far away you've always wanted to go?' I didn't answer, and he went on. 'Don't tell me where it is. But you decide, and after you pick up that letter, you be ready to go there.' And then he said, 'And listen, girlie. When you get my letter, take it back to your room before you open it, hear!' "

"Ye gods, mom! He wasn't kidding. Did the letter come?"

"Oh, yes. The next day. It was a plain manila envelope, stiffened with cardboard. Mailed from Holland and with no return address. That envelope nearly burned a hole in my hand all the way from the post office to my hotel room."

"What was in it?"

"Two thousand dollars."

I gasped, and my mom went on.

"Two thousand dollars in cash. Which was probably like five or six thousand today."

"Good night! Was there any explanation?"

"Just a note. It said, 'Don't blow it. There isn't any more.' " My mom gave a deep sigh. "I think that little note scared me more than anything else."

"It sure sounded final. What did you do?"

"I paid my hotel bill and packed my bags. I hid the money here and there in my suitcase, in my purse, and in my bra. The next morning I walked to the bus station. I looked the destinations over and bought a ticket to Dallas."

I laughed. "You mean you became a Texan on a whim?"

"Oh, I was far from becoming a Texan at that point. Dallas had a romantic sound to me. Cowboys and all that colorful stuff. I didn't necessarily intend to stay forever. That just happened. Or your father just happened. He was from a real Texas ranching community. I was bowled over because he could ride a horse."

"Daddy may be able to ride a horse, but he hates to!"

"I found that out later. When I met him I thought he was John Wayne."

I thought about my dad — tall, slim, ruggedly handsome. But no romantic cowboy. In fact, he doesn't like either horses or cows very well. Daddy's just interested in motors — trucks, cars, and boats. Suddenly I saw what a disappointment Prairie Creek must have been to my mom. She must have moved there expecting the Old West. Instead she found Blah City — a dull and colorless narrow-minded town on the prairie. No trees but mesquites, nothing more cultural than a small public library, and three thousand people who talked through their noses.

"You must have thought Prairie Creek was the end of the earth," I said.

We spoke in unison, quoting an old Texas joke. "It's not quite the end of the earth, but you can see it from there." Then we both laughed.

Again, a small laugh had broken the tension, and we rode along silently for a few miles. Mom was the next one to speak. "I've always wondered where that money Van Hoosier sent came from."

"It could have come from his own bank account."

"I wouldn't have expected a small-town law enforcement official to come up with that much."

"Oh, Van Hoosier could have." I quickly sketched the signs of the ex-sheriff's financial well-being.

Mom's voice was surprised. "But where did he get all that money?"

I thought a minute before I answered. And the answer to her question became clear — at least in my mind.

"I believe," I said, "I believe that he must have gotten the money from the McKay family. I have a feeling he got a lot of the money he had from the McKay family."

"If he did," Mom said, "I'm sure the McKays were smart enough to cover their financial tracks. We'll never be sure."

"Maybe not. But I think I know someone who might give us a lead."

"Who's that?"

"The man who was county attorney at the time you left Warner Pier. Joe knows him very well, and he's a sweetie. His name is Mac McKay."

"McKay!" I should have realized that Mom would be aghast. I spent the rest of the trip to Warner Pier — which wasn't very long — explaining to her that this McKay was one of the good guys, but that he knew a lot about the people he called his "rich relatives." Of course, I assured her that I would talk to Joe and to Hogan before I called Mac McKay, but she didn't know Joe and Hogan as well as I did, so that wasn't calming.

At least the discussion made the time pass quickly. We pulled into Aunt Nettie's drive before it was over. Joe parked behind us.

The next hour was spent greeting Aunt Nettie, and getting Mom settled into the bedroom that had once been hers and which was now the guest room. I had to try on my dress for Mom, of course. She approved and even shed a few tears. Then we went downstairs, and Aunt Nettie asked her if she thought it would be a good idea to paint the fireplace wall of the living room an "accent" color.

"Maybe crimson," she said.

"No!" Mom and I yelled in unison.

Then Hogan showed up for dinner. Mom had never met Hogan, of course, and she'd met Joe only briefly when we'd gone to Dallas at Christmas. Joe suggested, quietly, that we let Mom get acquainted with Hogan before we described the episode at the air-port.

I wasn't sure about this at first, but after I saw how Hogan was charming my mom, I decided Joe was right. So it was over coffee and apple pie that we told the story of the nefarious events at the airport.

After the unbelieving reaction of the Grand Rapids police and the airport security, I was relieved to see that Hogan was taking the situation seriously. He didn't jump to the phone and call the FBI, but he didn't say I'd been a scaredy-cat either. He guided the questions toward Mom.

And she repeated the whole tale about why she'd run away thirty-five years earlier. Well, she did leave out the part about being stark naked when she and Bill got caught in the McKay master bedroom, but she told the rest of it.

"Oh, Sally!" Aunt Nettie said. "If only you'd called us. If only you'd called Phil." A few tears ran down her cheeks.

"I was simply too afraid," Mom said. "I didn't want to tell the whole story to my mother, and I was afraid of the sheriff." She turned to face Hogan. "I'm not sure I could analyze just how I felt that long ago, but I think that — even then — I was pretty sure that Bill hadn't committed suicide. Today, I'm sure he was murdered."

Nobody had anything to reply to that. It seemed pretty obvious to all of us, but no one had verbalized it before.

After letting that sink in, Mom spoke again. "I think that's the real reason I ran. I was afraid I'd be killed, too."

Hogan leaned toward the table and looked steadily at my mom. "I understand, Sally," he said. "You were just an inexperienced young girl. It's easy to see why you ran away. It may well have been the smartest thing to do. My question is: Why have you come back now?"

Mom looked as if she'd been slapped. She ducked her head, sighed deeply, and toyed with her coffee spoon before she finally answered. Even then she seemed to be speaking to her dessert plate.

"I guess I figured it was time to straighten everything out," she said. "Thirty-three years is long enough to be on the run."

Aunt Nettie patted her hand. "We all want to help you, Sally," she said.

That pretty well summed up the evening. Hogan took Mom into the living room to go over her story again while Joe, Aunt Nettie, and I did dishes. Then Hogan arranged for his night patrol officer to come by the house periodically, and he asked me to leave a light on in the upstairs hall. If anything at all happened, we were to call him immediately and to turn out that upstairs light as a signal that all was not well.

"I like this old house as well as you and Nettie do," he said, "but it's not real secure. I keep telling Nettie she needs either a security system or a yappy dog."

Joe and I, with Hogan's approval, agreed that we'd try to see Mac McKay the next day, if he could fit us into his Sunday schedule. Maybe he could tell us more about the McKay clan and how they might mesh into my mom's story. I still felt sure that Van Hoosier's money had come from them.

Joe offered to stay overnight, saying he could sleep on the couch, so he could hear if anybody prowled around outside.

I laughed. "Like that yappy watchdog Hogan recommends? How loud can you yap?"

He wiggled his eyebrows. "I'm really more of a lap dog," he said.

Aunt Nettie spoke then, and her voice was firm. "Lee and Sally and I need a night to have some girl talk," she said. "You men just run along."

Actually, Aunt Nettie went to bed pretty soon after Joe and Hogan left, but Mom and I did wind up with some girl talk. Which, considering how poorly the two of us communicate, was probably the most unusual part of the entire evening.

Mom even initiated it, knocking softly at my door after I thought she'd be sound asleep. I heard her whisper. "Lee, are you still awake?"

"Come on in," I said. "I'm too keyed up to sleep."

She sat on the edge of my bed, as if ready for a mother-daughter chat. Then she didn't seem to know how to start.

"If you've come for a talk about the birds and the bees," I said, "I have to tell you that you're a little late."

Mom smiled. "Oh, I know you're a grown woman, Lee. But sometimes I wonder if I'll ever get to be one."

"I wouldn't say you were doing so bad, Mom. What brought this on?"

"That comment you made about my running away from everything."

"When did I say that?"

"When you called and asked me to come for the wedding."

"I didn't mean anything by it, Mom. At that point I didn't even know that you'd left Warner Pier on what should have been your wedding day."

"Nettie didn't tell you?"

"She told me later. But she'd never realized that I didn't know. So she hadn't brought it up."

Mom sighed. "Whatever you meant by it, I guess that comment broke the camel's back for me. I'd become aware long ago that I dodged all the problems in my life. I guess I'd hoped that you hadn't noticed."

"I hadn't."

"It must have been hard to miss. First I ran away from Warner Pier."

"Mom! You were young! After what Van Hoosier said, how could you stay?"

"That was my excuse at the time, but looking back I see that it was my responsibility to come back, to see that justice was done for Bill. I'm sure he didn't commit suicide, and I should have told the whole story to someone besides Van Hoosier, someone who would have listened."

"But even Bill's mother told you to stay away."

"Yes, but I think she meant for just a day or two. It was Van Hoosier who told me to go away and stay away. Anyway, I ran. Then I got resettled in Dallas, went to airline school, got a job, and two years later I met your dad, and we got married."

"And you got pregnant with me, and he dragged you to a town you never wanted to live in."

"I guess I was running away then, too. We had so many financial problems." She sighed. "I thought we could live within our income in Prairie Creek. Of course, your dad would never be able to live within his income. If he earned a million a day, he could spend it."

She sighed. "But I learned to live with financial uncertainty. It was Annie I ran from when you were in high school."

"Annie? Was Daddy seeing her before you left?"

"If you didn't know about it, Lee, I'm sure you were the only person in Prairie Creek who didn't. I'm glad to learn I was successful at keeping it away from you. But didn't you ever figure out why I packed you off to Phil and Nettie that summer?"

I shook my head. I felt as if I'd been kicked. I'd always blamed my mom for my parents' divorce. I thought she'd left because she hated Prairie Creek. To learn that she left my dad because he was involved with another woman — well, it rocked me.

Mom patted my hand. "I guess I shouldn't have told you. It's pointless, now that J.B. and Annie are married."

"Why do you say that you ran away from her?"

"Looking back, I guess I should have tried harder to keep your dad. Tried to cut Annie out."

271

Now I patted her hand. "If things had been right between you and Daddy, Mom . . ."

"She wouldn't have been a factor? Or if I'd cared more, I'd have been willing to fight for J.B.? Fifteen years after the divorce it's hard to say. Certainly there's no going back now." She smiled. "There've been a few more times I ran that you didn't know about."

"Hal Mead?"

"Oh? You knew about Hal? He did ask me to marry him, but I was too chicken. And there were a couple of other guys — ones who might have gotten serious if they'd had any encouragement."

"It's not too late! You're a very attractive woman."

She patted my cheek. "You're the beautiful one. That's why I wanted you to do the pageants, so everyone could see how beautiful and smart you are."

"Smart? You thought I was smart?"

My mom looked surprised. "Of course. You're extremely intelligent, Lee. I've always known that."

"I thought you . . ." I was too choked up to go on.

"You thought what?"

"That you believed I was dumb."

Mom gasped. "Oh, Lee! You're not dumb! You talked early, you did well in school, you've always been very quick to catch on to what people were up to. I never thought you were dumb!"

"I always thought you wanted me to be beautiful because you thought I was too dumb to get along on my brains."

"Oh, Lee!" Mom stood up and put her arms around me. I realized that tears were running down my face. "Sweetie! I was so proud of how beautiful you are — and maybe jealous."

"Jealous?"

"Yes. I was never pretty. I was always short and dumpy. I simply couldn't believe I had a daughter who was gorgeous. I guess I wanted to show you off. I wanted the whole world to recognize how beautiful *and* smart *and* talented you are! That's why I wanted you to win those silly crowns."

I wiped away my tears and tried to laugh. "Like the Scarecrow's diploma?"

"What do you mean?"

"In *The Wizard of Oz,* the Scarecrow wants a brain. Of course, all through the story, the Scarecrow is figuring out how to solve all the problems. He's the smartest character in the movie, but he doesn't see it. So the wizard — instead of giving him a literal

273

brain, gives him a diploma. The Scarecrow is no smarter or dumber than he was before, but now he has a symbol of intelligence. Maybe you thought being Miss UT Dallas would be my diploma."

Mom laughed. "Maybe I did. At any rate, you were a beautiful and gracious Miss UT Dallas, and I was proud of you. And when you called to invite me to your wedding — whether you knew why I left Warner Pier of not — you made me realize that I had been running away from a lot of things in my life. And I've vowed not to do that anymore. The pattern was set when Bill sent me away, then was found dead. And I'm going to try to set the record straight on that, as a beginning of my new way of life."

She hugged me again, and this time I hugged her back. We were still in this unaccustomed position, demonstrating mother-daughter affection, when I heard the noise outside.

CHAPTER 19

Mom apparently heard the noise, too. We whispered in unison. "What was that?"

"I don't know," I said, "but you call 9-1-1, and I'll turn out the hall light."

Mom picked up the wireless phone beside my bed, and I slid into the hall and flipped the switch. When I came back inside the room, I turned off my bedside lamp, then knelt by the window and peeked over the windowsill.

Mom was still on the phone. She put her hand over it and whispered. "Do you see anything?"

"No. I'm going to feel like an idiot if that was a raccoon trying to get the birdseed. I'm going downstairs."

"I'm coming with you."

There was a night-light at the top of the steps — they built stairs steep in 1904, and Aunt Nettie has a fear that someone will fall. I turned it out as we went by. Mom and I crept down, opened the door at the foot of the stairs, then tiptoed around the corner into the kitchen. We could see out those windows without having to twitch a curtain or lift a shade.

The snow on the ground reflected the moonlight and the big outside light the neighbors kept on all night, over behind the bare trees that marked the boundary between the lots. So there was a sort of aura outside.

Nothing unusual was visible from the kitchen window, but I heard that odd noise again. It was coming from the east side of the house, the side that overlooked the driveway.

I moved into the dining room. Mom trailed along, murmuring into the telephone now and then. We each picked a window and peeked around the edges of the shades.

For a moment I didn't see anything. Then I saw a movement beside Mom's rental car. A dark figure loomed against the light gray vehicle. I kept my voice low. "There. By your car."

"I see him," Mom said. "Who can it be?"

"Let's keep quiet. Maybe the patrol car will get here before the guy disappears."

The figure stayed beside the car, bent nearly double. I tried to see how large the person was, but it was hard to tell.

"I'm sure I locked that car," Mom said.

Suddenly a light came on, and Mom and I both gasped. The intruder had opened the driver's door and was leaning into the car.

The dome light shone like a spotlight on a dirty white stocking hat with a red pom-pom.

I gasped again. "It's Lovie!"

I'd kept my voice low, but Lovie straightened up as if she'd heard me. Then she trotted down the drive and disappeared around the front of the house. I ran to a living room window, but there was no sign of her.

"She's cut through to the Baileys' house," I said.

"Who did you say it was?" Mom sounded completely mystified.

I realized that I hadn't told my mother about the changes in Mrs. Dykstra's personality and position in the community, and even in her name — changes that popular opinion linked to the deaths of her younger son and her husband and to the banishment of her older son, Ed.

I sighed. "It's a long story," I said. "Tell the nine-one-one operator the person has run off, and let's make a pot of coffee."

But seeing Lovie had changed one thing

about the situation. I wasn't scared anymore.

When I'd heard the strange noise, when I'd realized someone was prowling around Mom's rental car, butterflies had begun to do a fandango in my stomach. After all, someone had tried to kidnap my mother that afternoon. Had they come again, ready to snatch her or to kill us all in our beds? Yes, I'd been scared.

But I couldn't be afraid of Lovie. She simply seemed too harmless.

Between Mom and me talking and the arrival of the Warner Pier patrol car, Aunt Nettie was also up within a few minutes. I did make a pot of coffee — I knew my mother was a genuine coffee hound, even ready to settle for decaf — and we gave the patrol officer some after he'd looked around the house and Mom's car. He found no sign that anything had been put into or taken away from that car. He didn't find any sign of Lovie either.

Then he left, and Aunt Nettie and I told Mom the whole story of Lovie's sad life.

Naturally, the story made Mom cry. "I can't believe this," she said. "Mrs. Dykstra was such a gracious, intelligent woman. To think she's become the town oddball — it's just too hard to take in. If only I'd come back after she told me Bill had committed suicide!"

"Sally," Aunt Nettie said firmly, "you're not to blame yourself for what's happened to Lovie Dykstra. She was a grown woman. She's responsible for her own life. She told you to go away."

"I'll have to see her," Mom said. "If she'll see me. Maybe she blames me for everything that happened."

"Wait a minute here!" I said. "Before we get all worried about Lovie and her feelings and what she thinks, let's find out what she was doing prowling around this house, breaking into your car."

"You said you felt sure she was harmless."

"That was my first reaction. But what was she doing? I think Hogan and his crew ought to look into it. And her presence reminds me of a second question — one we haven't really explored."

Mom looked wary. "What's that?"

"You said that when you and Bill got caught at the McKay cottage, his brother Ed was there."

Mom nodded slowly. "Ed wasn't the only person there. I heard at least three voices. But the only two people I actually identified were the McKay boy — the one I ran into on the porch — and Ed Dykstra."

"What connection would Ed Dykstra have had with Quinn McKay?" I said.

"They knew each other as kids. Ed and Bill helped their dad at the cottage sometimes, and all of them used to swim at Badger Creek Beach. Actually, Ed and Bill knew Quinn pretty well — at least in the summer. But I hadn't heard Bill say anything about him for a couple of years before that."

"Did Ed ever mention him?"

"Not in my hearing. But I didn't know Ed very well."

"I hope Mac McKay will talk to Joe and me about that side of his family," I said. "Maybe we'd understand a little more then."

We finally got in bed about two a.m. I was still asleep when Joe called at eight thirty and said Mac McKay had agreed to go out to lunch with us.

"You called him early enough," I said.

"Oh, he's a Presbyterian deacon. I knew I had to catch him before early church. He likes the contemporary service. You know, with guitars."

"When do we pick him up?"

"We don't. He'd going to meet us at Herrera's at eleven thirty."

"Mac drives?"

"You betcha. In the daytime, at least. And he seemed delighted to have an excuse to come over and have lunch in Warner Pier."

We both laughed. The cultural gap between Warner Pier — with its reputation for being more sophisticated and artistic than the rest of Warner County — is a joke to Joe and me. Despite its art galleries and upscale restaurants, Warner Pier is still a very small town, in mentality as well as in population.

"I'll meet you at Herrera's," I said. "I'll try to be a few minutes early."

Herrera's is one of three Warner Pier restaurants owned by Mayor Mike Herrera. Unlike the Sidewalk Café, it's quite formal — white linen tablecloths, velvet draperies, heavy silver, and an extensive wine list. It's one of the places we "sophisticated" Warner Pier-ites take out-of-town guests because it's elegant. Besides, the food is good.

Joe and I were waiting inside the front door by eleven fifteen a.m., and if we hadn't been a bit early Mac McKay would have beaten us there. He pulled up in a pearly white Cadillac, looking so small that I was surprised he could see over the steering wheel, and hopped out energetically. He was dressed in Sunday morning formal — dark overcoat, leather gloves, and plaid scarf. He beamed at us as he came in the door. "I hear the Bloody Marys are really good here," he said. "Will they leave out the silly celery stalk?"

"If they don't, I'll take it out personally," I said. I gave Mac a kiss on the cheek. "Thanks for coming."

"Joe said somebody's been bothering your mother," Mac said. "I've still got a streak of chivalry alive. If I know anything that will help, it's yours."

Joe had already snagged a corner table, so we settled Mac there and ordered Bloody Marys all around. Mac smiled gleefully and rubbed his hands together. "Now, what can I do to help you?"

Joe leaned toward Mac and dropped his voice. "I guess we want you to rat out your relatives."

"If you mean the Chicago–Warner Pier side of the McKay family, we parted company long ago. What I know about them may not be reliable. We're not well acquainted."

"You said that Quinn McKay worked for you one summer."

Mac nodded. "The summer before he was kidnapped."

"And you said he and his father didn't get along."

"That's mainly gossip. Quinn never complained. He never talked about his dad at all. But I heard from people who knew them over here on the lakeshore that there was a long history of Ben making fun of Quinn, sneering at him."

I asked the next question. "Why? What was wrong with Quinn?"

"Nothing that I could see. I thought he was a nice young guy. Smart."

"How did he happen to do an internship with your office?"

"Quinn was in prelaw at the University of Michigan. He wrote me a letter asking if my office could give him a summer job. I managed something for him. His father thought he should have been at some big Chicago firm, if he was going to condescend to take a summer job. So Ben wasn't happy, but Quinn and I got along fine."

"What was the problem between Quinn and his father?" Joe asked.

"I'm not even sure there was a problem. Like I say, a lot of this was gossip. But the story is that Quinn was one of those meek, quiet little boys — the ones who get bullied on the playground. One version was that as a kid he was afraid of the water, and Ben the Third was a big sailor — he always had a boat in the Chicago to Mackinac Race.

He apparently didn't like having a son who hung on to the mast instead of hauling up the jib — or whatever you haul up on a sailboat. The fact that Quinn was a good student didn't make a big difference to his dad. Ben was a rough-and-ready, break-the-rules type. He would probably have preferred a son who looked at the world the way he did."

"How did the mother fit in?"

"Benson the Third was a serial monogamist; he was married four or five times. Quinn was his only child, but I don't think his mother had been around much."

"And there was a new stepmother every couple of years?"

Mac nodded. "Right. Awful way for a kid to grow up."

"How did the father react to the kidnapping?"

"Oh, he handled everything according to the rules. What family there was huddled up at the Chicago apartment. They supposedly worked closely with the FBI." Mac leaned over confidentially. "Of course, anything I heard was secondhand. But I had a good source."

"He didn't pay a ransom?"

"No, Quinn managed to escape — or else the kidnappers let him go. The whole thing was never clear, not even to the FBI — or so I hear. But it was definitely a Patty Hearst copycat case, you know. Quinn was darn lucky he survived."

Joe spoke. "As I recall, some student radical group claimed to have kidnapped Quinn. Had he been mixed up in the student demonstrations at Ann Arbor?"

"Not that I know of. But Quinn probably wouldn't have confided his political opinions to me," Mac said. "He never said anything about Vietnam, for example."

"By the summer Quinn was kidnapped, Vietnam protests were pretty well finished," I said.

"Right. I always figured that was why the people who kidnapped Patty Hearst had changed their focus. There was no war to protest, so they claimed they were fighting poverty and injustice."

"I never could figure how either the SLA or Quinn McKay's kidnappers thought holding people for ransom would help their cause," Joe said.

"I never saw it either," Mac said. "Anyway, Quinn worked in my office that one year. He stayed at the McKay cottage over here and drove to Dorinda every day. I asked him to come back the next year, but he wrote and said his dad had arranged an internship in Chicago. I guess Quinn had gotten the rebellion out of his system by working for me that one summer. He said his father and current stepmother were going to Europe for the summer, so the Warner Pier house wasn't going to be opened. He didn't think he'd be up that year at all."

"And it turned out to be the most exciting summer of his life," I said.

"I liked Quinn," Mac said, "and his kidnapping bothered me. Of course, it was way out of my jurisdiction."

"Where did it happen?"

"Quinn was kidnapped in Chicago. He'd been staying in the family apartment there. And he resurfaced on a country road near Mount Vernon, in downstate Illinois. Nobody ever figured out where he'd been held. He claimed he escaped while being transported in a car.

"The screwiest part is, nobody had noticed he'd been kidnapped until the first ransom note came in the mail."

"How awful! Hadn't the office where Quinn was working noticed he was gone?"

"It happened on the weekend. Of course, none of this was known at the time. It wasn't all over the television like the Patty Hearst case. The FBI jumped in and kept it quiet. It didn't become public until Quinn turned up around Labor Day."

"How long had he been gone?"

Ed shrugged. "A couple of months by that time."

The calendar in my head began to click over. "Wait," I said. "If Quinn was found the first week in September, and he had been gone for around two months . . ." Mac nodded.

My heart began to pound, and I whispered. "That would put Quinn's kidnapping back to July."

"Right," Mac said. "It was the Fourth of July weekend, as I recall. I'd have to check that, of course."

Now my heart was really pounding. "But my mom's wedding — what would have been her wedding — was the last weekend in August."

Ed and Joe looked at me blankly.

"Don't you see? Mom says she saw Quinn McKay standing on the porch at the Warner Pier house on the day before what would have been her wedding day."

Joe frowned. "So?"

"So if Quinn was kidnapped in July, what was he doing walking around on the porch at the Pier Cove house in August?"

Chocolate Chat:
1970s Chocolate

When I quizzed my three children about chocolate memories from the 1970s, all of them said the same thing.

"Chocolate Soldiers at Grandmother's house."

Before any visit from her grandchildren, my mother (the one who gave me "choc") would stock up on Chocolate Soldiers, a chocolate milk soft drink. She believed it was healthier for children than regular soft drinks.

To the children, a soft drink in a bottle was much more grown-up than milk taken from the refrigerator and embellished with Hershey's syrup or Nestlé's Quik. (These were the dull chocolate drinks offered at home.) Chocolate Soldiers were exotic and only available at Grandmother's house in Arkansas.

A check of the Internet finds current references to Chocolate Soldiers. Apparently the soft drink is still available.

The soft drink Chocolate Soldier, of course, has quite a different flavor from the Chocolate Soldier cocktail — a concoction featuring gin, Dubonnet, and lime.

— *JoAnna Carl*

CHAPTER 20

I thought I'd really come up with something, but Joe and Mac McKay didn't react. They both just stared at me.

"How could Quinn have been there?" I said. "A free man. At least Mom didn't mention anything about his being bound and gagged."

Mac leaned forward, frowning. "That would imply that Quinn was a party to his own kidnapping," he said. "If he didn't seem to be a prisoner."

"It's hard to believe," Joe said. "Sally could have been mistaken. She said she didn't know him very well. It might have been someone else."

I pulled out my cell phone. "There's no point in arguing about it. I'll call and ask her." I hit the speed dial code for Aunt Nettie's house.

But the phone just rang. Nobody picked it up, and Aunt Nettie and I don't have an answering machine.

"That's funny," I said. "Mom and Aunt Nettie weren't planning to go anywhere. Maybe Hogan took them out to lunch."

I punched the code for Hogan's cell phone. He answered immediately, using his abrupt police chief voice. "Hogan Jones."

"Hogan, it's Lee."

Before I could go on, he broke in. "Lee. Great. I need you here at the station."

"I'm at Herrera's. We haven't ordered lunch yet."

"Order it to go and come right over."

"Sure. Hogan, this isn't about Mom and Aunt Nettie, is it?"

"No. Why did you think that?"

"I called the house, and they didn't answer. I thought maybe they'd gone somewhere with you."

"No. I've been investigating your alarm in the night. I haven't talked to them."

"Then where are they? Why didn't they answer?"

"I can't guess the answer to that one. One is in the shower and the other is sweeping the porch? They drove down to take a look at the lake?"

I didn't say anything, but my unease must have gone floating through the telephones, because after a second or two Hogan spoke again. "I'll send Jerry Cherry out to check on the house. But I do need to see you here. Now."

"Okay." I clicked the cell phone off and looked at Joe and Mac hopelessly. "I guess you guys are on your own for lunch. Hogan wants me to come down to the station. Something about the prowler we had last night. I'll try to get back."

I kissed Mac on the cheek again, put on my jacket, and left for the Warner Pier PD. Nothing in Warner Pier is very far away, so I didn't bother to move the van, and I walked to City Hall.

Since it was Sunday, the city offices were closed, so I went around to the back and went directly into the police department. Of course, it's usually closed on Sunday, too, but our prowler had apparently forced Hogan to open for business. I went in and closed the door behind me.

The first thing I saw was Lovie. She was sitting on a bench against the wall, wearing her old jacket and the white hat with the red pom-pom, the one I'd seen under the interior light of Mom's car. Her arms were crossed over her chest in a highly defensive posture, but her chin looked a bit quivery.

At least it looked quivery until she saw me. The sound of the door closing seemed to bring her out of a reverie, and her head popped toward me. But my appearance seemed to disappoint her.

She glared at me before she spoke. "I don't know what you're up to, little missy, but I wasn't anywhere near your place last night."

Getting into an argument with her didn't seem to be wise, so I just nodded and started toward Hogan's office, at the back of the room.

"Did you hear me?" Her voice was harsh. "I didn't mess with anything out at your house last night! I wasn't there!"

I still didn't answer, and she slumped down in her seat, pulling her head into her puffy jacket. She looked like one of the birds at Aunt Nettie's feeder, fluffing its feathers up to conserve warmth on a cold morning.

As I walked by she spoke once more, this time so low that only I could hear it. "I never wished Sally any trouble," she said. "I never wanted her to get mixed up in this."

I stopped. "In what? What didn't you want Mom mixed up in?"

Lovie only shook her head.

Hogan was standing in the door to his office, and he motioned me inside.

"I asked Lovie about last night, but she's not saying anything," he said.

"That hat is unmistakable," I said. "I'm sure that's what the person by the car wore."

"She's called someone — a lawyer, I guess. She says she won't say any more until he comes."

"We're not going to press charges," I said. "She didn't take anything and apparently the rental car isn't damaged. It's just that so many funny things have happened lately that I'd like to get at least one of them explained. Did Jerry find anything at Aunt Nettie's house?"

"He hasn't called in yet. But back to the business at hand — you're sure that you saw Lovie last night?"

"The light wasn't very good, but I saw her hat." He frowned, so I spoke again. "I'm sure about that. And Mom saw it, too."

A loud crash made us both jump; then we whirled toward the outside door. It had flown open and had banged against the wall. A hulking figure stood in the opening.

My jaw gaped. I didn't look at Hogan, but I'm sure his jaw was gaping, too. Lovie jumped to her feet. "There you are!" she said.

The hulking figure rushed across the room, leaving the door open, and grabbed her. It shouted, "Mom! Are you all right?"

My brain went into paralysis. Mom? This

hulking creature was calling Lovie "Mom"? If its dramatic entrance had surprised me, that development left me in a catatonic state. I couldn't move, talk, or — so it seemed — even breathe.

Hogan reacted more quickly. He strode across the office and closed the outside door.

At that point the hulk let go of Lovie and snatched off its stocking cap. He was completely bald.

Hogan spoke. "Ed Dykstra Jr., I presume."

He sounded calm, but I yelled. "He's not Ed Dykstra Jr.! He's Nurse Priddy!"

That seemed to surprise Hogan more than the hulk's dramatic entrance had. "Who's Nurse Priddy?" he said.

"He declared Sheriff Van Hoosier dead," I said.

"Van Hoosier?" Hogan sounded as confused as I felt.

The big man, whoever he was, unzipped his jacket and sighed. "Ms. McKinney is right," he said to Hogan. "I've been working at the Pleasant Creek Senior Center under the name Elmer Priddy. But you're right, too. My name originally was Edward Dykstra Jr."

Hogan looked serious. "You're the Dykstra boy who went to Canada?"

"Right. The draft dodger."

Hogan scratched his head, giving his Abe Lincoln impression. "Seems to me that the draft evaders were pardoned, given permission to come home, along in the Carter administration."

"Right. 1977."

"So where've you been?"

"I came back to this country in 1980. I went to Western Michigan and got my RN. I've been working various places since then." He still had his arm around Lovie, and he gave her a squeeze. "Mom knew where I was. We saw each other."

"But you didn't tell anybody else where you were? Or who you were? Why was that?"

Ed hesitated, inhaled deeply, then exhaled with a huffing noise. "I think I don't have to explain that right now. Right now I have to convince you that my mother didn't do anything to threaten Sally TenHuis and that she wasn't prowling around the TenHuis house last night."

"But I saw her," I said. "I saw the white hot — I mean, the white hat! I saw the white hat with the red pom-pom."

"You may have seen a hat like hers," Ed said, "but she wasn't wearing it."

We were still at an impasse. But of course Ed was right. I hadn't seen Lovie's face. I'd seen a figure, bent over and wearing a bulky, shape-disguising jacket, silhouetted against my mom's rental car. I hadn't been able to tell much about the figure's height, weight, age, or hair color. I'd identified Lovie strictly from her distinctive hat.

"I agree that it would have been easy to come up with a hat that would look like Lovie's," I said. "But why would anybody do that?"

"People harass my mom a lot," Ed — if that's who he was — said. "Maybe someone simply wanted to get her in trouble."

"But I never thought she was mixed up in that kidnapping attempt," I said.

Ed stared at me angrily. "She was definitely not involved in any so-called kidnapping attempt."

Hogan reassumed control of his police station then, cutting me off without actually using the words "shut" and "up," ordering Ed into his office, and telling Lovie and me to sit down and wait. "Keep quiet" was an unsaid part of his instructions. So I sat down, folded my hands, and stared into space. Lovie didn't say anything, so I thought a series of confused thoughts.

The appearance of Ed — who had apparently been in contact with his mother all along — was an unexpected twist. As I'd blurted out, I could never suspect Lovie of being mixed up in what I still believed was the attempted kidnapping of my mother. She simply wouldn't have been able to get hold of a large and impressive car to use in the plot. And she didn't have an available driver.

Unless Ed — I pictured the driver who had tried to snatch my mom. He'd worn a furry hat and a dressy overcoat. But no, he wasn't Ed. He'd seemed familiar, true, and I was still trying to place him. But he wasn't Ed.

And how did all this link up to the death of Sheriff Van Hoosier? Of course, Ed — in his persona of Elmer Priddy, RN — had been present when Van Hoosier died. But Ed had been the one who insisted Van Hoosier's death had not been natural. Even though his boss, the nursing home director, hadn't liked it — even though Van Hoosier's doctor might have let Ed declare the ex-sheriff dead without a personal check of the body — Ed had insisted that Van Hoosier had been bashed and then smothered. Which pretty much let Ed out as a suspect.

Lovie had been at the nursing home the day Van Hoosier died, too. Joe and I had seen her leaving. That thought gave me a chill right between my shoulder blades, and

I sneaked a peek at her. She was sneaking a peek at me.

I closed my eyes and tried to picture Lovie as a killer. At first the thought seemed really silly. Lovie was an old woman. But she was an old woman who got lots of outside exercise, walking along Warner Pier's streets and the rural roads of western Michigan, picking up cans. And I'd seen her toss huge sacks of those aluminum cans into the back of her truck. Yes, she might have had the strength to smother a man who had been weakened by a stroke.

Lovie spoke suddenly. "Ed blames himself, but it was my fault!"

Her voice startled me, and I opened my eyes so quickly that I nearly yanked a crick in my eyelids. I didn't say anything.

"My fault!" She repeated the words, and they almost became a wail. "My fault! I was the one who lured him into that world. I was the one who thought we might accomplish something. It was all my fault."

She needed soothing, but I didn't know what would calm her down. We stared at each other for at least thirty seconds before I spoke. "I'm sure Chief Jones will sort it all out," I said.

My comment didn't have the desired effect. "Chief Jones! He's probably as big a crook as that sheriff was!"

Lovie pulled her padded jacket around her as if she were in a strong north wind. She began to rock back and forth. She gave a loud sniff and wiped her nose with the back of her hand.

I had to respond to her sorrow. I took two Kleenex from a box Hogan's secretary kept on her desk and sat down by Lovie. "Let's trust the chief as long as we can," I said. "He's a really smart man, and I think he'll do his best to understand everything that's going on."

"Ed's all I have left," she said.

"I know." I put my hand on her arm.

"And he's good!" Her voice became loud again. "He would never have killed anyone! He would have saved his brother if he had known!"

Her words made me feel as cold as she looked. Here was confirmation that Ed had been mixed up in whatever happened to Bill Dykstra, in the crime that had sent my mother fleeing to another part of the country, afraid to come back to her hometown.

What did Lovie know about that? I leaned forward to ask her. As I tried to formulate the question, I heard the Warner Pier PD radio, broadcasting from a corner of the office. I didn't understand all the police jargon, but I recognized the voice as coming from Jerry Cherry. And he sounded excited.

Jerry Cherry? Excited? Jerry was the patrolman the chief had sent out to Aunt Nettie's house to make sure she and Mom were all right.

I listened. The chief had apparently picked up the mike he kept in his office, but I could hear both ends of the conversation.

"What's going on?" Hogan asked.

"Chief, I got here, and two cars were in the drive, but I couldn't find anybody," Jerry said. "I walked all around the outside of the house. Nada. Then I tried the back door. It wasn't locked, so I went inside. Yelled out who I was." He took a deep breath. "And Mrs. TenHuis answered me. Way far off."

"Where was she?"

"Chief, she was locked in the basement! The door had been jammed so that she couldn't get out. She says a guy wearing a ski mask put her down there. And he must have taken Lee's mom away. She's not here anywhere!"

CHAPTER 21

It's hard to explain how I wound up fleeing the police station in Lovie's old truck.

"Fleeing" isn't the right word, of course. When Jerry Cherry broadcast the news that Aunt Nettie had been locked in her own basement and my mom was nowhere to be found, the four of us who heard it leaped to our feet like a chorus line hearing the cue to go on stage, though each of us sang a different song.

Hogan yelled, "Is Nettie all right?"

Ed Dykstra rushed out of Hogan's office, slamming the office door back against the wall with a crash.

Lovie called out plaintively. "Ed?"

I ran for the door.

But Ed beat me. He didn't stop to answer his mother, and he came by me so fast that it's a miracle I wasn't knocked over by the wind. If I had fallen, he would have trampled me into the tile floor of the Warner

302

Pier PD and not even noticed. I followed him out as quickly as I could, but Ed was jumping into his small SUV by the time I reached the sidewalk.

I stood there, bouncing from side to side, realizing that my van was at Herrera's. I heard Hogan's patrol car revving up, back in the PD's parking lot. Its siren began to blare, and I realized I was too late to get a ride with Hogan. I'd have to run several blocks to get transportation.

Then Lovie came scuttling past, headed for her beat-up old truck. So I didn't hesitate. I climbed into the passenger side without asking permission. Lovie barely gave me a glance. She just started the truck, threw it in reverse and shot out of her parking place.

I started to call Joe to tell him what had happened, and I realized that I didn't have my purse. I'd left it in the police department, on the floor under my chair. So I didn't even have my cell phone.

I was riding with the town's crazy woman, nobody knew where I was, and I had no way to contact anybody who might want to know. I considered asking Lovie to let me out, but she was heading in the direction I wanted to go, so I kept quiet.

Hogan's siren was rapidly fading into the

distance, but Lovie's old truck was noisy, so I had to yell at her. "Do you have a cell phone?"

She shook her head, but she didn't look toward me.

I fastened my seat belt. I could only assume Lovie was headed to Aunt Nettie's house.

Lovie seemed to be a good driver, though she was ignoring the speed limit. She went tearing down Peach Street, turned onto Dock Street, then crossed the Orchard Street Bridge. After she swerved onto Lake Shore Drive, I could see the spinning lights on top of Hogan's car a quarter of a mile ahead of us, and we could hear his siren. As long as we were following Hogan, I wouldn't feel threatened.

Hogan slowed and turned into Aunt Nettie's lane. I assumed Lovie would turn in after him. But Lovie went right by.

I grabbed her arm. "We needed to turn there!"

She shook her head so hard the red pom-pom on her hat bounced like an apple on a McIntosh tree hit by a strong wind. "We've got to save Sally!" she said. She drove on, looking straight ahead, completely intent on the road.

The siren had stopped, and I tried yelling

over the truck's noise again. "Where are you going?"

"To get Sally away from those awful men!"

"Which awful men!"

"That Quinn McKay!"

"Quinn McKay?" I gulped that one down. It didn't come as a big surprise. I was convinced my mom had seen Quinn McKay at his family home — walking around free at a time when he was supposed to be a hostage — and she'd heard at least two other men talking. I didn't stop to wonder who the third might have been.

Lovie was muttering. What was I doing, barreling along Lake Shore Drive in a truck driven by a crazy woman?

"Yes, Quinn McKay was in it," she said. "And Ratso."

"Ratso?"

"Ratso! The one I thought was my friend. The one I trusted."

Lovie seemed to be grinding her teeth. She sounded crazier than ever. "The one I should have told on years ago. But I had to protect Ed."

Who could she mean?

I yelled again. "Where are we going?"

"Where they've taken Sally. Pray that we're not too late. They've already killed two people. She's got to be there!"

"Where?" I yelled out the question, and Lovie turned her head toward me for half a second. "Why, the McKay house," she said. Her tone implied that I must be a complete idiot not to know.

I sat back. If Quinn McKay was one of my mom's kidnappers, I supposed that taking my mom to his family cottage had some logic. But Lovie wasn't making sense, and I was sorry that I'd ever got in her truck.

"Oh, it's all my fault!" Lovie was still muttering. "I got them into it. Ed and Ratso! I thought it was a good idea."

"You thought what was a good idea?"

"The protests. But it turned out to be a bad mistake. Ratso ramped up the whole deal. I told them it was stupid. I thought I'd talked them out of it! Then they killed my son!"

"Did they kidnap Quinn McKay, too?"

"Kidnap? Ha!" Lovie was slowing now. I could see the hulk of the old white house, the McKay place, back in the woods. Was she going to turn in?

"Mrs. Dykstra! Lovie! We should go to the police! Turn around and go to Aunt Nettie's house."

"No," Lovie said. Her voice was quiet, but firm. "No, I've got to go here. I've got to face them down, make them turn Sally loose."

She swung into a lane marked by a mailbox with a cheerful red cardinal painted on it. Then she stopped, blocking the drive.

"We get out here," she said. "You can go back to your aunt's house. It's best if I go on alone."

She got out of the truck and started slogging on up the drive.

I gaped a minute, then I slogged after her. If my mom was being held at the McKay house — a claim I didn't accept — it was the last place in the world for a crazy old lady.

"Lovie — Mrs. Dykstra! Let's go back to the truck. Let's call the police. If the kidnappers are there, the police should deal with it."

"No! I should deal with it. It's all my fault."

Lovie slogged on, head down, picking her way through really nasty snow — snow that had melted and refrozen a dozen times on a driveway that had not been plowed all year.

I didn't know what to do. Should I slog after her? Slog back to Lake Shore Drive and find a phone? Lots of the houses along there were closed for the winter. It wouldn't be easy to find one. I might have to hitchhike. But would I dare accept a ride, with kidnappers on the loose? I might have to slip and slide for more than a mile — clear back to Aunt Nettie's house.

I obviously should have run down to pick up the van instead of jumping into Lovie's truck. Time spent running two blocks on Warner Pier's cleared sidewalks would have saved me time that I needed more now.

But I simply couldn't let a crazy old lady go off to a deserted house in the Michigan winter by herself. I told myself that Hogan was looking for my mother. As worried as I might be about her, I couldn't really do anything at Aunt Nettie's house. And I might be able to persuade Lovie to get back in her truck and give up this trek to the McKay house.

Because I considered her story about the kidnappers being there completely ridiculous.

So I followed her up the long drive that led to the McKay house, listening to her mutter about everything being her fault. I talked, too, but our conversation wasn't logical.

"I believed we could change things," Lovie said. "But not this way. Not this way!"

"Come back to Aunt Nettie's with me,

Mrs. Dykstra! We'll let the police handle this."

"I should have spoken out years ago, but it might have meant Ed's life! I couldn't bear to lose both my sons."

"Please come back with me, Mrs. Dykstra."

"I thought Sally was safe, as long as she didn't come back!" She turned to me and spoke angrily. "Why did you make her come back?"

"I didn't! I —"

But she grabbed my arm and gave a mighty "Shh!" We'd come around a line of evergreens and were within sight of the house.

"Be quiet!" Her voice was an order. "They mustn't hear us."

I whispered, but I pleaded with her. "Mrs. Dykstra, come away. You can see that the house is deserted. All the shutters are up. There's no one here. If you think the house should be investigated, we'll ask Hogan Jones to do it."

I was wasting my breath. Lovie walked on toward the house, and I trailed helplessly in her wake, like a dinghy being pulled along by a scow.

This was the first time I'd ever seen the house clearly, since it was completely hidden by foliage nine months out of the year and was only a ghostly shape in the bare woods in the winter. It wasn't a showplace, as so many of the summer homes along the lakeshore are. It looked more like a big, roomy farmhouse. It was surrounded by an acre of snow and had evergreens as a background, but the heavy shutters nailed over each window kept the house from looking like a Christmas card. It didn't look welcoming; it looked cold and ominous.

The snow around it was unbroken by human tracks. The porch was covered with drifts, and the cellar door was so snowed in that I could barely see what it was. As we approached the house, the only unshuttered opening I could see was a side door that led onto an extension to the porch — a sort of deck. I realized that that must be the door to the bedroom, the one my mom had fled through thirty-three years earlier.

Lovie hadn't let go of my arm. She clutched it and motioned toward the north side of the house. She was still whispering. "We can get in through the kitchen."

"Lovie! We can't go into the McKay house! We're trespassing already."

I might as well have kept my mouth shut. She kept her grip on my arm and slogged forward.

Now we were off the drive, fighting our way through unbroken snow, rounding the big square white house. I gave up the argument. We didn't have a key to the house, so we couldn't get in without smashing the back door. When Lovie saw that no one was at the house, she'd surely agree to go back to Aunt Nettie's with me.

But as we reached the north side of the house, I got another surprise. Lovie hitched up her ski jacket and reached into the pocket of her flannel-lined jeans. She pulled out a key. A key that had been discolored by age.

Lovie gave a guttural laugh. "Ed Sr. always told Ben he needed to change the locks on this place," she said. "Neither he nor this fancy-pants wife who inherited ever got around to it."

Using a finger to caution me to silence, she stepped onto a broad back porch. As I followed her, I looked down to make sure where the step was.

That's when I saw the footprints.

They led around the other side of the house, up the steps, and onto the back porch. My eyes popped. I could see two sets of larger tracks — men's boots, I'd guess. Then there were marks that showed skidding and sliding.

And there was one clear print of a woman's shoe.

Had the kidnappers brought my mom here?

While I'd been gaping at the tracks, Lovie had silently crossed to what must have been the kitchen door. She tried the handle, then put the key in her jacket pocket.

The door was already unlocked. As Lovie opened it, I could hear voices.

Lovie was right. The kidnappers had taken my mom to the old McKay house. She had been fighting, trying to get away, as they dragged her to the back door. But she'd been alive. That one clear track showed she'd reached the back door on her own two feet.

As soon as I reached that conclusion, I questioned it. After all, the McKay house wasn't at the end of the earth. It was only a mile and a half away from Aunt Nettie's, in a civilized — if lonely — neighborhood. And even though the house had been closed for the season, that simply meant the heat wasn't on, the water had been cut off, and there were shutters on the windows. As Lovie had just demonstrated, it was possible to go in and out at will, and there was no reason members of the McKay family wouldn't do that anytime they wanted. I couldn't identify the track of my mother's shoe; the track on the back porch might have been made by a McKay wife, daughter, or girlfriend.

I slipped in the back door behind Lovie and stood in the kitchen, still doubtful.

But then I heard a voice, and it shattered any idea I had that Lovie and I had walked in on an innocent gathering.

"Look at the candles flicker!" a raspy voice said. "Somebody came in!"

Another man laughed jovially. "Don't be stupid! Nobody could know we brought Sally here."

And I knew who Ratso was.

CHAPTER 22

"My initials spell a word," he'd said at the council meeting. "That means I'm lucky with money."

Raleigh A. Taylor. Retired teacher, city councilman, tightwad, and all-around civic volunteer with a strange smile.

It made perfect sense. Rollie had known Lovie; they'd been student activists at Western Michigan. He'd known Ed Dykstra — also a student activist — through Ed's mother. Ed had been at the University of Michigan, and so had Quinn McKay. And Quinn and Ed had been childhood friends.

And if Ed, Quinn, and Rollie decided to fake a kidnapping, either to raise funds to fight pollution or just to fight their own poverty, Benson McKay III — head of a company they regarded as a major polluter — would have been a logical person to cough up the ransom.

And they couldn't have found a better

hideout than the McKay cottage, closed for the summer because Quinn's dad and stepmother were in Europe. Quinn would have had a key, and Ed would have known how to get hold of his father's key, plus he'd have been familiar with his father's routine for checking on the cottage.

All this flashed through my mind, and it must have left me as limp as an old sock, because when Lovie put her hand on my shoulder and gently shoved, I knelt on the spot. Obeying her gesture, I ducked down beside a large kitchen range.

I thought she wanted both of us to hide, but Lovie didn't get down with me. And I was barely on my knees when the light changed, and I realized a door must be opening.

Because of the shutters, it was dark in that kitchen, but I could see that a candle was being poked into the room. It cast weird shadows on the face of the man who held it.

I pulled my head farther back behind the range, something like a turtle retiring into its shell, but I could still see Lovie, standing close to me, in front of the stove.

A gruff voice spoke. "What the hell are *you* doing here?"

"I knew you had to be here when I heard

315

that you'd taken Sally," Lovie said. "Where is she?"

"Sally's not hurt. But how did you know where we were?"

"Ed told me."

"Ed? But he's gone."

"Ed's come back! He didn't know you'd killed his brother!"

"I didn't kill him!"

Lovie spoke right over him. "Ed didn't even know Sally had run away! And Sally doesn't know anything! Or she didn't! Why did you take her?"

"We can't take chances."

"You're being silly, Quinn!" Lovie raised her hand, then slapped it on top of the range, rattling it as she emphasized her words. "Let Sally go!"

The door swung open wider — I could see the top of it — and a different man spoke. "Well, if it isn't the one who taught us the three Rs," he said. "Rioting, rallies, and revolution."

If I hadn't already figured out who it was, I would have recognized the dumb joke. The second man was Rollie Taylor.

Lovie spoke again. "I didn't teach you kidnapping and murder. You got into that for your own reasons."

"Yeah, and your precious Ed got into it,

316

too." This came from the man with the big nose — was he really Quinn McKay?

"Ed had nothing to do with murder," Lovie said. "And Sally had nothing to do with anything. She knows nothing that can threaten you. Let her go. Where is she?"

Rollie laughed. "Sally liked that fancy cathouse bedroom so well — back when she was almost a bride — that we put her in there again. But this time we made sure she couldn't get to the outside door."

I could see the top of the door move again. "Come on in the living room," Rollie said. "We've got a little fire. We need to know about Ed. Where is he?"

"I don't know," Lovie said.

The candle was withdrawn, Lovie went with Rollie and Quinn, and the door closed. I was in the dark, stuck behind the kitchen stove. But Rollie and Quinn didn't know I was there. Now all I had to do was call the cops, rescue my mom, and escape.

Ha.

Thanks to the shutters on the windows, the kitchen was pitch-black. The kidnappers were in the next room, and nothing but an old-fashioned swinging kitchen door separated me from them. If I made a noise, they'd hear me. The back door was unlocked, but if I went through it, the draft would make the door swing and the candles flicker, just as it had when Lovie and I came in. So if I went out that way, I'd have to run like heck, through deep snow, on a bright, sunny afternoon. I could almost guarantee that Quinn and Rollie could run me down before I could get to the road. Unless they had a gun. That would make it even easier for them.

Lovie had kept Quinn and Rollie from knowing I was there, but she'd also left me in an impossible position. I had to get out of that kitchen and it wasn't going to be easy.

I stood up slowly. The bad guys' candle, which had almost seemed to glare while Quinn was sticking it through the door, had dazzled me. Now my eyes were slowly adjusting to the darkness, and I realized that it wasn't as complete as I'd first thought.

There was a soft glow around that swinging door, for one thing. And one of the shutters didn't fit exactly right. A line of light showed down the side.

If only that light would shine on a telephone.

I realized that a kitchen might well have a telephone. And I knew that most people who had summer cottages didn't bother to disconnect the telephone for the winter;

they'd simply have to pay to hook it up again in the spring. I began to look around. Was there a phone sitting on the counter? A phone hanging on the wall?

I spotted it. It was a vague shape on the wall, near the swinging door. I moved across the kitchen floor slowly, carefully, praying that my wet boots wouldn't squeak. Lovie was haranguing Quinn and Rollie loudly. I realized she must be trying to cover any noise I might make.

I reached the phone. Oh, wonderful instrument. It could connect me with Aunt Nettie, with Hogan, with rescue. I eyed it hungrily.

It was a portable phone.

Damn. While the standard, old-fashioned phone is independent of the source of electrical power, this one wouldn't be. It relied on electricity. And the electricity had been off in this blankety-blank cottage for months. There was no point in even picking that phone up.

I turned around in disgust and headed back toward the stove, still creeping along slowly, carefully. My eyes had adjusted to the gloom now, and as I got to the range, I saw something on its top.

A key. It was the key Lovie had produced, the one she'd planned to use to get in the back door. When she'd whopped her hand on the top of the stove, she must have left that key.

That was nice of her. But what the heck good would it do me? I didn't want to lock anybody inside the darn cottage. And the back door was already unlocked. I could go out any time I was willing to cause a draft.

But if I could get outside, I realized, I could go in another door — such as the side door, the door off the deck, the door to the room where my mom must be a prisoner.

But how could I get out of the kitchen and around the corner to that door?

Then I remembered I'd seen another door as Lovie and I came around the house. A cellar door. The old-fashioned kind used when farmers carried potatoes or apples into the basement for winter storage.

And cellars traditionally were also accessible from kitchens.

I spotted a door at the back of the kitchen. My heart began to pound. Could it be my escape hatch?

I tiptoed back there — the argument in the living room was getting louder and louder — and I carefully opened that door, peeking around it to see what was inside.

Something flew out at me.

It was instinct that made me put up my

hand, some primitive instinct that I was about to get hit in the head and should try to avoid the blow.

I gasped and realized I was standing there holding a mop handle. I'd opened the broom closet, and the mop had nearly fallen out.

My heart was beating so loudly I felt sure Quinn and Rollie would hear it in the next room. It took me at least a minute of deep breathing to get my nerves calm enough that I could move.

When I was able to command my muscles again, I opened the door a bit wider and tried to see what else was in that closet. It might hold something useful. Like a flash-light.

I didn't find a flashlight, but I did see an odd white stick — right in front of me, at eye level, lying flat. Thanking my tall Texas and Dutch ancestors, the ones who handed me the genes that made me tall enough to see what was on that shelf, I touched the white stick gingerly. It was a candle.

It was beside a cheap star-shaped glass holder. And right beside the holder was an old peanut butter jar. Hope began to sing. I took the peanut butter jar out and held it in the light coming in around the shutter, and my heart gave a leap of joy. It held a box of matches, sealed inside the jar to keep out the damp.

I knelt behind the range again, opened the jar, and lit the candle. And once it was lit, I found the cellar door without any trouble. It was around a corner in a little alcove that held the refrigerator.

I crept down the cellar steps and found myself in a Michigan basement, a cellar with a sand floor and stone walls. By that time I was completely turned around, and I had to make a circuit of the cellar before I found the outside door. Then another fear arose. That door ought to be held shut from the outside by a padlock. I might need a hacksaw to get out. Or an ax.

But luck was with me. The double door to the blessed outside was held shut by a bar on the inside. A rugged two-by-four was across the double doors, held at each end by rough-hewn wooden hooks.

Some McKay farmer of bygone days had carved those hooks himself, and the family had never bothered to change the arrangement.

Not that it was easy getting out. Even after I'd taken the bar down, I had to shove on one of the doors like crazy, then dig my way out through the snow. I shoved the door just far enough open that I could squeeze out.

Then I knelt in the snow and panted for a minute before I reached inside and pulled out my candle.

I stood up and started for the side deck and the door to what Rollie had called the "cathouse bedroom."

Before I could get there, someone called my name.

I was completely surprised — I swear I looked up in the trees to find where the sound was coming from. Then I thought I'd imagined it.

But I heard it again. A low sound, almost a whisper, but insistent. "Lee!" When I looked around, I saw a movement.

It was Joe. He was standing at the edge of the woods, and he was motioning to me. I could see his mouth move. "Come! Come!"

I longed to run to him. Right through the snow.

Next I saw another movement, and I realized Hogan was standing about ten feet away from Joe. And through the bare winter trees, down on Lake Shore Drive, I saw police cars.

The police had found out where we were — even though I hadn't been able to tell them. They were surrounding the house.

I felt a great sense of relief. But it was quickly followed by fear.

My mom was still a prisoner in that house. She would be a hostage. When the police stormed the place, she'd be in desperate danger.

I had to get her out.

Joe was still gesturing. He obviously couldn't understand why I was just standing on the deck — holding a lighted candle in the bright sunlight — instead of running toward him.

I put the candle on the porch railing. Then I gestured to him. We'd gone to a couple of West Michigan Whitecaps games the summer before, and the entertainment had included audience participation. We'd all waved our arms enthusiastically, spelling out "Y-M-C-A" with gestures. Maybe I could remember the motions, and maybe Joe would recognize them.

I stuck my elbows up in the air and clinched my hands on top of my head. *M.* Then I made my arms into a big circle with my hands linked in the air above my head. *O.* Then I made another *M.* Then I pointed to the door behind me. I took Lovie's key from my pocket and pantomimed turning it in a lock. Then I picked up my candle and moved toward the door.

It might not open anyway, I told myself.

But it did. The key turned easily in both

locks — the one in the door handle and the deadbolt. I opened the door just a sliver, and I poked the candle inside.

I saw a movement. My mom was alive.

She was tied to one of the bedposts, and thank God she was gagged. I'm sure I startled her so much that she might have screamed. But she couldn't.

Putting my finger to my lips, I crossed to the bed. The floor was covered with a thick carpet, so making noise wasn't such a worry in there.

Then I started trying to get her loose. Rollie and Quinn had used some kind of clothesline to tie her up, and the knots didn't make any sense at all. I struggled with them.

Mom began to yank her head back and forth, and the light changed. I realized someone had come in the door behind me. It was Joe.

He pushed the outside door almost shut, and he crossed to the bed. I gave him the finger on the lip bit, and he nodded. He took a look at the knots that held my mom; then he reached somewhere under his ski jacket and produced a pocketknife.

It was more beautiful than a diamond tiara.

Joe's wonderful knife — as a good craftsman he takes care of his tools, so it was sharp — made quick work of the clothesline. We had Mom untied and off the bed in about a minute. We were holding her, trying to help her stand up and dragging her toward the door, when the noise coming from the living room changed.

First a loud bang came from somewhere in the house. It was wood against wood, and it was a hard blow.

Quinn yelled, "What was that?"

Rollie yelled, "What are you doing here?"

Lovie yelled, "Ed!"

Ed yelled, "Mom! If they've hurt you, I'll kill 'em!"

Joe growled. "Ed's come in without waiting for the rest of the troops," he said. He dropped Mom's arm and headed for the living room. Ed had apparently made his usual entrance, banging the door into the wall.

I jumped from side to side, trying to figure out what to do. I had to get my mom out of there. But I sure did want to know what was happening in the living room.

As I whirled around, trying to decide what to do, I spotted a big metal candlestick on the bedside table. I shoved Mom toward the outside door.

"Run!" I said. Then I grabbed the candlestick. Small objects flew from around its base, but I ignored that. Holding that candlestick over my head — and probably roaring some kind of war cry — I ran for the living room.

The scene in there was already confused. For one thing, the candles they'd been using had apparently fallen over and gone out, so the only light came from the fireplace. Ed Dykstra and Rollie were locked in combat. Lovie was hovering over them holding the fireplace poker. As I ran in she whacked Rollie on the shin.

But I didn't pay too much attention to them. Joe and Quinn were circling each other, fists doubled up. Or Quinn's fists were doubled. Joe — once a champion amateur wrestler — was facing him with bent knees and arms extended, hands half open and ready to grab him and tie him into a knot.

It was no time for a fair fight. I whammed Quinn on the shoulder so hard that I broke the heavy candlestick. He dropped to one knee, screaming.

"My god!" Joe said. "I hope you didn't break his shoulder!"

"I hope I did," I said.

Then I realized that Mom had run into the room. She was holding the candlestick that matched mine, the one from the other side of the bed.

She rushed toward Rollie and Ed, who were now rolling on the floor with Ed on top, and raised the candlestick like a club.

"Stop!" Joe and I yelled the word at the same time. "You're about to hit one of the good guys."

With Joe to help, Rollie was immobilized before Hogan and his cops rushed in through the kitchen door.

Hogan looked at the scene — Rollie pinned securely by Joe and Ed, Quinn just beginning to move, and Mom, Lovie, and me all brandishing clubs — and shook his head.

"And they complain about cops being violent," he said. "We're not in it, compared to angry civilians."

CHAPTER 23

Once I got a look at Quinn in the light, I recognized him. He was the well-dressed man who tried to pick up my mother in a big black Lincoln at the Grand Rapids airport. He was also the mysterious big-nosed customer — the one with his collar zipped up around his ears — who had bought a pound of bonbons and truffles from me three days before. Joe and I decided later that Quinn came into the shop so he could see what I looked like, in case he needed to know.

Quinn and Rollie, not being complete idiots, both hired lawyers immediately and have kept their mouths shut. There are signs, however, that Quinn's willing to cut a deal. He's obviously going to deny any involvement with the deaths of either Bill Dykstra or Sheriff Van Hoosier. And that could be true; Quinn could claim that he didn't know Rollie had killed Bill until after the fact, and he has already proved he was in Chicago on the day Van Hoosier died. Rollie, on the other hand, was at the retirement center that day, calling bingo. Now *there's* a suspicious activity if there ever was one.

Ed Dykstra is being frank with the authorities, or so he claims. Joe doesn't think he'll be charged with anything. If Ed left Warner Pier before Bill was killed — and Hogan thinks he's telling the truth about that — all they could charge him with would be attempted extortion from the failed attempt to force Quinn McKay's father to quit polluting Lake Michigan and to pay ransom. Because Quinn himself was involved in that effort — and he has since inherited his father's fortune — that whole case is in legal limbo. There might be a charge to do with wasting the time of law enforcement officials, but after thirty-plus years, it's hard to say. Ed's mainly concerned with trying to keep his license as a registered nurse.

I did witness an odd episode in the Superette, when Ed came face-to-face with Greg Glossop. Greg stammered out a greeting, looking terrified at the sight of Ed. Ed got a wicked grin on his face and acted very friendly. Then, as he said good-bye, he patted Greg on the shoulder.

"We were young in interesting times," Ed said. "But those times are long gone for both of us."

Greg looked relieved.

But just where did Sheriff Van Hoosier fit into the kidnapping of Quinn McKay?

Apparently, after Mom called and told Van Hoosier about finding Ed, Quinn, and the unrecognized — by her — Ratso at the McKay cottage, the sheriff saw a chance to make money off the McKays. So he ordered my mom out of town. Then he went to the cottage, where he found Rollie and Quinn, who must have been hanging around trying to make the fake kidnapping plot work.

Subsequent events indicate that, while Quinn's motive in faking his own kidnapping may have been forcing his father to stop polluting Lake Michigan, Rollie's — even then — was probably money. His tightwad attitude should have been a hint; money is really important to Rollie. That was a clue to his true character, I guess, just like the way he smiled at inappropriate times. I think the smile was a demonstration of the false face he showed the community for thirty-three years — doing good deeds outwardly, while he was blackmailing and murdering behind closed doors.

At any rate, since the time the kidnapping

plan was upset it appears that Van Hoosier and Rollie had combined their efforts to blackmail Quinn McKay. If Quinn's personality didn't still have elements of the meek little boy he once was, Rollie and Van Hoosier would probably both have died by his hand years ago. He must have hated and resented them.

But they were smart blackmailers, Hogan says. They didn't bleed Quinn too badly. Each of them asked for just enough to pay their living expenses — to buy groceries, clothes, other items that wouldn't raise questions when they were paid in cash. They could basically double their salaries with that technique, and the proceeds were tax-free. It was a simple method of laundering money.

Ed and his mother weren't in touch for a year after Bill died, and even after they began to see each other again, it took some time for them to pool their information. They had figured out that the sheriff was involved, because they felt sure some of the circumstances of Bill's death were covered up, but they didn't really understand what had happened.

Ed had no trouble with people recognizing him after he came back to western Michigan. All anybody seemed to remember about him was that he had a huge head of black hair and a large black beard; a razor and the passage of time changed his appearance drastically. He assumed a false identity before he entered nursing school.

But Ed says he'd never given up figuring out who killed his brother. After Van Hoosier moved to the Pleasant Creek Senior Apartments and Nursing Center, Ed sought out a job there, hoping to keep an eye on the old law officer.

Ed says he was stunned when he ran into Rollie at the center. Rollie was apparently also keeping an eye on Van Hoosier. Luckily, Rollie didn't recognize Ed. But when Rollie found out my mom was coming back to Warner Pier and that I was trying to find Van Hoosier, the old sheriff's fate was sealed. He had to die before Joe and I could question him.

Ed was eager to keep Joe and me interested in the link between my mom and Sheriff Van Hoosier, however. That's why he came by TenHuis Chocolade and told me the sheriff had muttered about my mom being connected to a kidnapping. Now Ed admits he made that up to keep our curiosity piqued.

A white knit hat with a roughly made red pom-pom was found in the McKay house after Quinn and Rollie were arrested. Apparently one of them disguised himself as Lovie — all it took was the hat and a big down jacket like hers — and came by to poke around in Mom's rental car. We don't understand why they did this. Nothing was taken from the car. My theory is that they intended to damage the brakes, but Joe thinks they were merely trying to get us to think Lovie was involved with all the odd goings-on.

As I say, it's hard to tell just what will happen by the time everything shakes out, but I do think that my mom will no longer be afraid to come back to her hometown.

And Lovie's still picking up cans, but she's washed her hat.

Nobody died at our wedding.

Oh, there were a few disasters — like Lindy scorching the hem of her dress at the last minute — but none of them were fatal. Of course, once my mom was saved from her kidnappers and we got her on the plane back to Dallas, I had tried to head off a few calamities.

First, I took Mercy to lunch and explained to her that my own mother was financially unable to help with the reception. I was frank. "My mother has no money sense," I told her. "She has no savings, no IRA. And you do. I know that, and I admire that, and I'm thankful for that. But how can I snub my own mother and allow you to give the reception?

"And Joe and I still don't want a rehearsal dinner. But I'll tell you what we do want. We'd like a Sunday brunch for all the family members before everybody heads out for their planes. Mercy, it would be a terrific help if I could turn that over to you."

Mercy beamed. "Of course," she said. "How many are we talking about? A dozen? Fifteen? I can handle that at my house — if Mike helps me cook."

"That would be wonderful. And I need another favor. Your guidance."

"Guidance on what?"

"On Warner Pier customs. For example, we really don't want to spend our money on a band. But could we have a deejay? Or would that look too fancy? Hot hors d'oeuvres? Or just wedding cake, punch, and a dish of nuts, like in Prairie Creek?"

Mercy beamed even brighter. And she was a major help. She suggested a keyboard player who performs in the Sidewalk Café bar during the summer. He played everything from hard rock to golden oldies. Perfect. She convinced Joe that a steamboat round would not only be too expensive, but also too pretentious. She suggested hand-written reception invitations — and she helped write and address them.

After I'd talked to Mercy, I tackled Aunt Nettie. I cornered her after dinner, and I tried to explain how much she and Uncle Phil had meant to me, how I had appreciated their taking me in when I was a difficult teenager. I thanked her for giving me a picture of what a truly happy marriage could be like, of what a real home is.

We were both in tears by then, but I went on.

"And your house is part of my picture of what a home should be," I said. "That's why I want to marry Joe here. Please don't change it, fancy it up. I love it just the way it is."

"It sure would be nice to have another bathroom," Aunt Nettie said. "And some decent closets."

"I'm not getting married in the bathroom! Or the closet!"

Then we both started laughing. But that ended the discussion of redecorating.

The month before the wedding, the hair-net ladies — the wonderful women who actually make TenHuis chocolates — surprised me with a shower and gave us a very fancy set of cookware. Lindy and my banker friend Barbara gave us a wine and cheese party with all the guys invited. The dishes, silver, and toasters poured in; I got way behind on my thank-you notes.

The ceremony itself was just fine. Joe told me I looked great in my champagne lace. He looked pretty good himself, even if he was so nervous he almost dropped the ring.

My dad escorted me down Aunt Nettie's steep stairs and kissed my cheek as he handed me over to Joe. His wife, Annie, and my mom smiled at each other and made it look sincere.

My stepsister, Brenda, seemed pleased to be asked to guard the guest book at the reception, and Tracy and Stacy, the two girls who wait on our counter during the summer, introduced her to a neat guy who thought her Texas accent was really cute.

My fellow foodie Margaret Van Meter made us a beautiful wedding cake, and Aunt Nettie laid out silver trays of scrumptious chocolates and bonbons. The flowers — pots of white hyacinths in massed arrangements — were beautiful, and everyone admired my wedding ring and my bouquet of yellow roses. Mac McKay had more fun than anybody, unless it was Joe's dad's mother, age ninety, who left her central

Michigan retirement home for the occasion. Mac brought Inez Deacon over from Dorinda. Lovie even got a new dress and had her hair done. People didn't recognize her. Ed had grown his hair back, so a lot of people did recognize him.

But maybe the gate-crasher caused the most comment. He was a nice-looking fellow — thinning white hair and a trim figure — and he appeared in the guest line, smiling a little shyly.

"Hi," he said, "I know I'm not invited, but I hope Sally McKinney will vouch for me."

"Jake!" Mom ran and gave him a big hug. "You said you couldn't make it!"

"I was able to shift some things around," Jake said. "I didn't want to miss this. It's special for you, and you're special to me."

Hmmm.

I didn't have time to find out a lot about Jake before Joe and I left on our honeymoon the next afternoon. Is he important to my mom? Or simply an escort? Has she quit running?

We hadn't planned on dancing, but somehow it began around eight and went on until midnight. Or so I hear. At eleven Joe and I went on to what had been his apartment and was now our home. And that was

338

perfect, too.

And the Sunday morning brunch went very well. Mike did omelets to order for anybody who wanted one, and Mercy made hot fruit salad and a coffee cake from her grandmother's recipe. She got out all her silver and china and reused some of our pots of white hyacinths.

Then, just before we were going to leave, Aunt Nettie and Hogan beckoned us into Mercy's bedroom.

"We wanted to give you your wedding present," Aunt Nettie said.

"You've already done that," I said.

Aunt Nettie's gesture brushed away four place settings of pottery as insignificant. Then she handed me a flat box wrapped in white paper and embellished with a shiny gold bow. It weighed hardly anything.

I took the wrapping paper off and opened the box to reveal a whole lot of tissue paper. Beneath the tissue was a photo of Aunt Nettie's house. I was puzzled.

"Keep looking," Aunt Nettie said.

Under the picture was a legal document. I immediately handed it to Joe. He read it.

"Oh, my god! Nettie, you shouldn't do this!" He turned to me. "She's deeding us her house!"

I was too stunned to speak, and Aunt Nettie was too tearful.

A lot of hugging and eye-wiping went on before she explained.

"The house is *yours*," she said. "You don't have to keep it the way it is. You can tear it down, add on to it — or sell it. It's just a piece of property, not a shrine."

"But you've lived there for more than thirty years," I said. "We can't put you out of your home."

"She won't be needing it anymore," Hogan said. He gave her a kiss on the cheek. "I've talked her into moving into my house. After we're married."

CHOCOLATE CHAT:
TWENTY-FIRST-CENTURY CHOCOLATE

The twenty-first century is bringing a new emphasis on chocolate in exotic forms. And one of the more intriguing offerings is the chocolate equivalent of a coffeehouse.

In a number of cities it's now possible to visit a chocolate lounge, marked by comfortable chairs and chocolate truffles and bonbons in exciting flavors. Drinks usually include coffee and, of course, hot chocolate.

I had the opportunity to visit a chocolate lounge in Chicago. Absolute bliss. Highly recommended for a relaxing hour. What's not to like about a cup of black coffee to contrast with a Ginger Citrus Truffle or a Mucha Margarita bonbon?

The healthy aspects of chocolate are being exploited, too. New dark chocolate bars contain bunches of flavanols that fight hypertension, dementia, and diabetes.

And one company is marketing a chocolate-flavored shake containing healthy fiber.

What next? Chocolate spinach?

— *JoAnna Carl*

ABOUT THE AUTHOR

JoAnna Carl is the pseudonym of a multi-published mystery writer. She spent more than twenty-five years in the newspaper business, working as a reporter, feature writer, editor, and columnist. She holds a degree in journalism from the University of Oklahoma and also studied in the OU Professional Writing Program. She lives in Oklahoma but spends much of each summer at a cottage on Lake Michigan near several communities similar to the fictional town of Warner Pier. She may be reached through her Web site at www.joannacarl .com.